# HELL TO PAY

A DETECTIVE KAY HUNTER NOVEL

RACHEL AMPHLETT

SAXON
PUBLISHING

ISBN eBook: 978-0-9945479-5-8

ISBN paperback: 978-0-9945479-4-1

ISBN audiobook: 978-0-9945479-6-5

# CHAPTER ONE

Detective Sergeant Kay Hunter leaned over the passenger seat of her car, plucked a pair of old leather ankle boots from the foot well, and cursed both the unfortunate motorist who'd lost control of his vehicle, and DI Devon Sharp for phoning her at one in the morning to attend the scene of the accident.

'Meet me on site in thirty minutes,' he'd said, before the line went dead.

She wiggled in her seat until she could slip off her flat shoes, exchanged them for the boots, and shoved the car door open before pulling her waxed jacket around her, gasping as rain lashed her face.

She squinted against the headlights from the emergency vehicles lined up along the hard shoulder of the motorway, an ambulance's blue lights flashing through the steady downpour and strobing off the windows of the patrol cars that were being used to cordon off the accident scene. Further along, two firemen returned from their truck, their faces grim as they stepped over the remains of the steel barrier and disappeared from sight down the embankment.

Blinking the last remnants of sleep from her eyes, she shoved her hands into her pockets and began to search for her superior officer.

When Detective Inspector Devon Sharp had called her, the shrill tone of her mobile phone had roused her from her slumber and caused her other half, Adam, to curse loudly before he rolled over and tugged the duvet over his head.

His snores had reached her as she'd crept out the bedroom door.

Now, she wished she'd put on another layer of clothing as she stalked along the road.

A vicious wind whipped across the exposed raised section of the motorway, the bordering fields providing no shelter from the change in season.

As she neared the ambulance, she spotted a uniformed police officer standing next to the open back doors, his face attentive on the activities around him. Kay realised the crew were inside and peered in, curious.

The pair worked as a well-rehearsed team, an older woman and a younger man who bent over their patient, their voices clipped.

Beyond, at the front of the vehicle, a radio crackled; a man's voice from their control centre at Ashford calm and efficient as he relayed information to the crew.

The scent of disinfectant reached Kay as she

watched them work, her eyes running over the once immaculate equipment while she wondered how long it would take them to clean the vehicle when they finally returned to base at the end of a long shift.

'He had to be cut out of the wreckage.'

Kay turned at Sharp's voice. 'What are his chances?'

'Head trauma. Suffered a cardiac arrest while they were bringing him up the embankment on a stretcher. So, not good.'

Kay shielded her eyes against the rain and bright lights and peered along the motorway.

An intermittent stream of transcontinental trucks and an occasional car drove past the cordon, their speed slowed by the warning signs displayed on gantries several miles before the crash site.

Surface water sprayed out from under their wheels, pooling at the road's edge where Kay stood. Despite knowing the cordon had been erected at a safe distance, she took a step back as a large truck swept by, the downdraught from it buffeting her slim frame.

'Any other vehicles involved?'

'No. Uniform are taking the statement of a truck driver over there – he was parked on the hard shoulder when the accident happened.'

They both turned at a call from the ambulance, and the younger of the paramedics stooped so he could talk to them.

'We've got him stabilised. We'll be off now.'

'Thanks,' said Sharp. 'Where's he going – Maidstone?'

'Yeah, that's where we've been told to take him.' The paramedic lowered himself to the ground and prepared to close the rear doors. 'I wouldn't hold your breath about him making it though.'

Sharp turned his attention to the young uniformed officer. 'Go with them. If he talks, I want to know about it.'

'Guv.'

The paramedic waited until the police officer had clambered in, then made his way along to the driver's door.

Kay and Sharp stepped out of the way as the vehicle manoeuvred away from the cordon before setting off along the motorway, its sirens blaring to clear a path between the trucks.

Kay watched it disappear into the distance, then stamped her feet and turned to Sharp.

Ex-military, he was impeccably dressed despite the time. Only his bleary eyes gave any indication of the fact he had also been woken in the middle of the night.

Kay narrowed her eyes as she realised he was even wearing a tie.

She felt scruffy by comparison.

'Come and take a look,' he said, failing to notice her discomfort, and led the way towards the edge of the embankment.

The other emergency services had set up two floodlights at the top of the hill to enable the fire crew to work to free the driver of the vehicle. Saving his life had taken precedence over preserving the scene for the crime scene investigation unit, and Kay could well imagine what the lead investigator would say when he saw the state of the undergrowth.

Large footprints led down from the roadside, and as Kay reached into her pocket and switched on her torch, the beam highlighted the total devastation left by the vehicle's path, followed within an hour by a team of first responders.

'What's their initial thoughts about what happened?'

'According to the truck driver parked back there, he saw the car veering to the left in his mirrors – thought it was going to hit him. Seems as though the car driver tried to correct it at the last minute, but lost control and sent himself spinning through the barrier. Traffic have already taken a look at the point of impact and traced it back – there's oil on the road, plus the grease from the past two weeks.'

Kay nodded. After a particularly dry end to the autumn, a sudden deluge had lifted all the grime from the roads and created hazardous conditions for unsuspecting motorists.

Avoiding the broken edges of the barrier, they moved to a spot that wouldn't block the team's egress from the broken vehicle to the motorway and stood for a moment, watching the activities below.

'What made Traffic call it in as a murder scene?' Kay called over the howling wind.

In reply, Sharp held his hand out for her torch before walking a few more paces until he was at a different angle to the car and swept the beam over the back of the vehicle.

A pale arm snaked out from the boot and over the rear licence plate at an impossible angle.

'Her,' he said.

# CHAPTER TWO

Sharp stepped closer to the barrier and whistled to the crime scene team below.

One of the white suit-clad figures straightened at the sound, then pointed to its right and up the bank.

'Good. Harriet's got a demarcated path set up at last.'

They pulled on overalls and booties from a box of supplies left next to the barrier, the thin material flapping in the wind against their own clothes, and then Kay tied her hair back and followed Sharp down the slope, mindful of the fact that if she wasn't careful, she'd slide on the wet undergrowth and scoot down the rest of the way on her backside.

The floodlights provided enough light to move safely along the path, so Kay shone her torch to her right, tracking the path the vehicle had carved through the vegetation as it had plummeted to where it now lay.

She'd seen some bad road accidents in her time with the police service, and gave a low gasp as she cast her eyes over the destruction.

'It's a wonder he lived, isn't it?' said Sharp over his shoulder.

'Yeah. He must've been thrown around like a rag doll.'

As they drew closer to the foot of the embankment, Kay noticed that a wire fence separated the Highway Agency land from that of a farmer's field.

The landscape beyond the outer reaches of the floodlights appeared as though it had been abandoned since harvest time, the earth laid fallow and bare.

Kay shivered as a cold gust of wind buffeted her and rocked the gantries from side to side, then turned her attention to the crash site.

She could only imagine the mammoth task that faced Harriet's team – it was only now the driver of the car was on his way to hospital that the investigators could do their job. Their task would be exacerbated by the fact that at least twelve other people had traipsed through the now-cordoned-off area since the crash.

A tent had been erected over the back of the vehicle while she and Sharp had been talking at the top of the embankment, and as Kay drew closer she could see Harriet standing off to one side, calling out instructions to her team while they propped up a second tent over the driver's door of the car. A photographer moved from one side of the car to the other, the flash from his camera illuminating the scene in bursts of light that bounced off the trunks of nearby trees and cast silhouettes amongst his colleagues.

Harriet glanced over her shoulder when they approached the cordon, and then made her way towards them, her progress hampered by tree branches and thick vines that covered the mud-strewn ground.

'Evening, detectives.'

'Harriet.' Sharp jerked his chin towards the vehicle. 'What've you got so far?'

The crime scene investigator pulled her paper mask down. 'Female, mid-twenties by the look of it. Wrapped in a black plastic sheet that was taped together. Bruising to the face, which obviously wasn't caused by the accident – not enough time has elapsed. I can't see any bindings around her wrists. I'll let Patrick finish the preliminary photographs, and then we'll take a closer look.'

'Thanks.'

Sharp fell silent as Harriet replaced her mask and returned to the small tent, her white suit covered in splatters of mud from the knees down.

Kay sniffed the air, a heady mix of spilt fuel and the earthy tones of the nearby field. She glanced back up the embankment at the sound of air brakes, and spotted a large tow truck pull up to the barrier, its hazard lights flashing. She checked her watch, and wondered if they would be finished in time before sunrise.

The last thing they would need was for the crime

scene to slow down the morning commute and end up on the news before they could work with the media team to coordinate a structured response.

On the other hand, to rush the forensic examination of the vehicle while it was still in situ would be a disaster. The next few hours were crucial for capturing as much evidence as possible.

The photographer moved closer to where Kay and Sharp stood, then lowered his camera.

'Okay, Harriet, I've got all the preliminary photographs,' he called over to the car. 'Anything else you need from the perimeter?'

'No, that's fine. Let's get a move on and find out what we've got. Charlie, can you move one of those floodlights closer?'

A technician moved away from the group, slapped a colleague on the arm as he passed and pointed away from the car, before the two figures grabbed hold of the nearest floodlight and shuffled their way towards the rear of the vehicle.

Once satisfied the lighting rig had been secured so the wind wouldn't blow it over on top of someone, Harriet set to work once more.

Kay held her breath, the temptation to lift the tape between her and the vehicle tempered by the knowledge that she couldn't simply impose upon Harriet's work.

From their position at the cordon, Kay had to crane her neck to try and see what Harriet was doing.

The woman spoke to her team as she worked, her low voice carrying on the wind as she pointed to different parts of the vehicle and set her colleagues to work taking samples and placing everything in evidence bags to begin their arduous task of recording every minute detail.

After half an hour, Harriet lifted her head from the back of the car and beckoned them over.

'All right, come and take a look.'

Sharp lifted the tape so he and Kay could pass underneath it, and led the way to the car.

Her eyes roamed the vehicle as she drew closer, the dents and scrapes caused by the velocity of the crash even more evident under the harsh bulbs of the gantry lights.

She left Sharp to speak with Harriet while she circled the car, surveying the damage to the panel work.

The passenger door had been ripped off its hinges and lay further up the embankment from where the vehicle had finally stopped, a steady stream of debris tumbling amongst the undergrowth as three of Harriet's colleagues hurried to collect as much of it as possible before the wind seized it.

Rounding the back end of the car, she joined Sharp beside Harriet.

He stepped to one side and gestured to the woman's body. 'She didn't stand a chance.'

Kay lowered her gaze.

The woman appeared to be in her twenties, her naked form wrapped in the black plastic before being dumped in the back of the car.

Harriet had snipped away at the tape that held the

plastic together, exposing the woman's bruised and battered body. Cuts and welts covered her left cheekbone and eye socket, her face twisted away from them.

'We'll finish here and get her to Lucas as soon as possible,' said Harriet. 'Though bear in mind we have to take samples from the whole car and gather everything from its path of travel. We'll be here a while yet.'

'Understood,' said Sharp.

Kay shifted from foot to foot and ignored the damp starting to seep through the protective bootees and into the leather uppers of her boots. 'I can't recall any similar cases to this one, can you, guv?'

'No. That's what worries me.'

She turned to face Sharp. She was almost the same height as him, but he stood a little further up the slope to her and so she had to lift her chin. His face was troubled.

'You think he's done this before?'

'Maybe.'

'Perhaps it's a one-off, a domestic case.'

He shrugged.

Kay sighed and faced the car once more.

No matter what Sharp thought, their first priority would be identifying the driver and his victim before working out where they had travelled from.

And where he had been taking her.

The thought that they might have missed a practiced killer with several burial sites spread around the county town sent a shiver down her spine.

What if he hadn't crashed?

When would he have been caught, and how many other victims would there have been?

'He'd better survive surgery,' she muttered.

# CHAPTER THREE

The next morning, bleary-eyed from lack of sleep, Kay glanced up from her computer at Sharp's low whistle, and then wheeled her chair over to where the rest of the investigating team were beginning to gather.

She nodded to Detective Constable Carys Miles, whose dark hair hung to her shoulders – a new style for her, and one she'd confessed to Kay she was only trying for the coming winter months.

'It's too damn hot in summer for long hair,' she'd grumbled. 'But at least I can keep my neck warm now.'

Kay had laughed at the comment – she felt the cold chill of winter as early as late September, and would never contemplate having her blonde hair cut shorter than its current length. Her only compromise was to keep her fringe short so she could at least see what she was doing on a day-to-day basis without it getting in the way.

Gavin Piper and Ian Barnes, two more detective

constables, joined them, the younger of the two – Gavin – choosing to perch on a nearby desk, his notebook and pen poised ready.

He'd passed his exams the previous month with flying colours and was now a firm part of the investigative team at the county town's police station. Naively, Piper had thought his colleague's teasing would stop the moment he was no longer a probationer, however Barnes had other ideas, especially as the tall handsome man was the gossip of the female members of the administrative pool of staff and was known to spend most of his free time surfing off the Cornish coastline. He kept his blonde hair regulatory length, but it still had a habit of sticking out in tufts due to the amount of salt water it had been exposed to over the summer months, accentuated by the deep tan that still clung to his skin.

Kay viewed the older man, Barnes, as the glue within the team.

Barnes could be relied upon to lighten the mood when required, but also commanded an enormous amount of respect amongst the assembled detectives and administrative staff. In his mid-fifties, he'd been a police officer since he was in his twenties and his knowledge of the local area and its history had been relied upon time and again when Kay had worked alongside him. He'd confided in Kay that he'd started dating someone before the summer, a conveyancing solicitor he'd met through friends, and it seemed the romance had blossomed.

Kay picked up her notebook and pen, flicked to a clean page and settled into her seat as Sharp began.

'Right, for those of you who weren't on scene last night, I'll give you a quick update,' he said. He pinned a series of colour photographs of the crash scene to the whiteboard beside him. 'At ten past eleven last night, Traffic were called to a car accident on the M20 about quarter of a mile past the Harrietsham exit. When they got there, the driver was unconscious, but still alive, and fire and ambulance crews worked to free him from the wreckage and get him to hospital. He's currently at Maidstone Hospital in an induced coma after six hours of surgery.'

He paused to let the team catch up with their notetaking, and then pinned a further three photographs to the board.

'In the back of the car, the body of this woman was found.'

A silence filled the incident room as the team stared at the photographs.

'The hospital has confirmed they've had to remove the driver's spleen, and I'm told he also has a broken leg and will require further surgery to pin that in due course. They're keeping him in the induced coma to try and reduce the swelling to his head wound – looks like he banged his skull against the window of the car when it rolled down the embankment.'

'What are his chances?' said Kay.

'Grim, but as soon as we get confirmation from the

hospital he's conscious, we'll be making arrangements to formally interview him.'

A murmur swept through the incident room. It would make their jobs harder if they couldn't question the driver, and although none of them wished him ill health, they also wanted to see justice served for the man's victim.

The DI waited until their voices had quietened. 'Carys – has anything come up on the Police National Computer about the car registration?'

She shook her head. 'There's nothing that looks like a connection, guv, but some of the records on the database from the Driver Vehicle and Licencing Agency are a mess, so I've put in a request to them. It doesn't appear to be a hire car, though. Hopefully I'll get some clarifying information from them soon.'

'All right. In the meantime, fingerprints were taken from the driver, but we've drawn a blank,' said Sharp. 'He doesn't appear in our system. He had no wallet or identification on him, and none were found in the car. Two mobile phones were located in the car, however, and those have been passed to Andy Grey's digital forensics team at headquarters. We would've brought them into evidence here, but they were crushed in the accident, and we needed Grey's expertise to extract what information we could from them. Harriet's team found another phone amongst the undergrowth that had the female victim's fingerprints on it. Grey confirmed fifteen minutes ago that the last call made on one of the phones in the car was made to the victim's phone.'

'But why would he be calling her?' said Barnes. 'He knows where she is – in the boot of his car.'

'Maybe she's known to him and he called her before killing her?' said Kay.

'Or it was a hit and run?' said Gavin. He shook his head. 'No, that doesn't make sense.'

'What about the woman? Any information about her?' asked a female police constable on the fringe of the small group, her pen poised.

'None. Again, her fingerprints have been taken, but she doesn't show up in the system, Debbie,' said Sharp. 'So, can you circulate the prints to our colleagues in Sussex, Essex and the Met to start off with to see if they have anything for us? Widen the search if they don't. Lucas Anderson is planning to do the post mortem tomorrow morning, so we'll have to wait to see if that turns up anything to help us by way of dental records and the like.'

'Will do, guv.'

Debbie West regularly supported the major crimes unit, and Sharp always sought her presence from the uniform staff at the station if she was available.

Diligent and one of the most talented users of the HOLMES2 database the team relied upon to manage any investigation, Debbie exuded a degree of calm amongst the often fraught team dynamics.

Sharp's attention returned to the detectives. 'While Debbie's following up the fingerprints angle, Carys – you and Gavin start working with Missing Persons to see if our victim turns up on those databases. Harriet emailed some photographs from last night's scene, so you can use those. Again, widen your search if she doesn't show up in Kent.'

'Will do.'

'While Carys is dealing with the DVLA, we need to trace where that car's been,' said Sharp. 'Gavin – get on to the ANPR. Have them trace the car from its last known point on the M20 to its starting point. Tie it in with local CCTV and see if we can pinpoint the driver's movements.'

'Guv.'

'Carys – speak to uniform. As soon as Gavin has a starting point, we're going to need their help. Could be industrial, could be residential but it's going to take manpower. I'll speak to DCI Larch about the budget.'

'Kay, Barnes – the minute we have an identification for the driver, check the database to see if we have a note of him in the system and any known acquaintances. No doubt we'll be paying some of them a visit over the coming days, so I'd like to have an update on where we can find them. In the meantime, you can help Gavin by going through the local CCTV footage when we get it.'

'Got it.'

'Right.' Sharp checked his watch. 'We'll have another briefing at five o'clock. Let's see what we've managed to pull together by then.'

# CHAPTER FOUR

Kay wandered over to the water cooler and filled up two white plastic cups before joining the small group around the whiteboard at the far end of the incident room.

The winter sun had dipped below the horizon over an hour ago, the sky turning from pale grey to black within minutes.

Kay checked her watch. She'd forgotten to eat, and hoped the final briefing of the day would be short.

'Here you go,' she said, and handed one of the cups to Barnes.

'Thanks.'

Supervisors for the team responsible for reviewing the ANPR and CCTV images were present, as well as a number of administrative staff from headquarters who were tasked with liaising with the uniformed officers.

Kay yawned, the packed incident room quickly becoming stuffy due to a combination of temperamental central heating and lack of ventilation. She and the rest of the team had been running on coffee and adrenalin all day, and despite her best efforts, exhaustion was beginning to seep in.

Sharp blew a loud single-note whistle to bring the numerous muted conversations to a halt, and everyone turned their attention to the front of the room where he stood.

'Thank you. Debbie – can you dim the lights, and I'll take you through the images we've got from the cameras.' He hit a remote switch, and an aerial view of Maidstone appeared on the wall beside him, the projector's light catching the shoulder of his jacket as he moved to one side. 'My thanks to our uniformed colleagues who have worked all day to pull this together for us. We'll start with the crash site and work backwards. As you can see from the image here, we've got a lot of area to cover.'

Kay fought down the tiredness, knowing she had to stay focused. Whoever the driver was, she wouldn't relax until he was convicted and put away for a very long time.

The ambient light in the room dipped and wavered as Sharp switched to the next image.

'This was taken as the vehicle passed below the bridge under the railway,' he said, and continued to change the images as he commentated, using a laser pointer to trace the details. 'The driver left Maidstone via the A229 to join the motorway. Prior to that, we have CCTV placing him here.'

His audience leaned forward as one.

On the screen was a grainy image of the vehicle passing along an empty street, but only the front grille of the car showed.

'Where's that, guv?' said Gavin.

'Wheeler Street. Runs off Holland Road. Unfortunately, the contractors responsible for maintaining the CCTV cameras along there haven't been keeping to their schedule, and we're missing at least twenty minutes.' He flicked to the next image. 'At present, we have no idea where the vehicle was between this prior known position here on the A26 to where we've spotted it in Wheeler Street.'

'That's enough time to kill and hide a body in the car,' mused Kay.

'If that's where he killed her, yes. Part of uniform's remit tomorrow morning will be to speak to business owners along Wheeler Street and Holland Road to see if anyone's got some camera footage to help us. If they have, we'll try to fill in the gaps using the information to hand.'

Despite Sharp's optimism, Kay could hear the underlying frustration. It was a long and laborious task and in the meantime, they'd be treading water waiting for the results.

'Moving backwards,' said Sharp, 'we have the car pinpointed at a roundabout at Mereworth. He disappears then, again due to lack of camera coverage, and we pick him up here, on the outskirts of Tonbridge – his starting point.'

A darkened street appeared, its kerbs lined with a variety of cars outside tightly packed terraced houses.

'We'll have teams of uniformed officers mobilised in the morning to assist with door to door enquiries in Tonbridge,' said Sharp. 'The first team will be out early to try to catch as many people as possible before work or school commitments. A second team will set out at six o'clock to go to those houses we get no response from during the morning session. All statements will be entered onto the system by the administrative staff at headquarters as they come in from the teams in the field. Kay, Carys – as soon as we have confirmation from the door to door enquiries which house that vehicle belongs to, I want you to do the formal search at the property. I'll get the necessary warrants authorised, but it means you're going to have to join the team in Tonbridge tomorrow morning so you can act immediately. We'll get Barnes or Gavin to get the search warrant to you. Might be a good idea for you to tag along with uniform, speak to the neighbours to give yourselves a head start.'

'Guv.'

'I'll have Harriet and her team on standby to conduct a forensic search.'

Kay nodded, but didn't respond. If it transpired the woman had been murdered at the property, the whole place would be locked down immediately while the crime scene investigation unit worked their way through the building.

Sharp switched off the projector, and tossed the laser

pointer onto the desk next to him as the lights were switched back on.

'Right. See you tomorrow, everyone. Don't be late.'

# CHAPTER FIVE

Kay emitted a sigh as she extracted herself from the car, the late night and subsequent early morning start finally catching up with her.

Adam, her partner, had parked his four-wheel-drive on the gravel driveway rather than in the garage outside the house he'd inherited from a grateful elderly client, and she had to squeeze between the two vehicles to get to the front door.

She noticed the back of the four-wheel-drive was open, so she changed her mind and sidled down the side of the vehicle until she reached the garage, and then made her way through to the kitchen via an internal door.

Adam was crouched on the floor with his back to her, a boxlike wooden structure on the floor beside him. He glanced over his shoulder as she shut the door behind her.

'Hi,' he said. 'I thought I heard your car on the driveway.'

He straightened, and Kay tilted her face up to his before he kissed her.

She lowered her gaze to the balsa wood structure. 'What is it this time?'

He grinned. 'Something you'll really like. Cute and fluffy.'

He ran a hand through his unruly black hair, his eyes sparkling.

Kay peered around him, and realised the box was in fact a small hutch with an enclosed area at one end, and a wire mesh covering the other half. Adam had spread newspaper out under the open end.

Adam moved to the kitchen bench and rummaged in a plastic carrier bag, before turning back with two ceramic bowls in his hands. He handed one to Kay.

'Do you want to fill that one up with water? It's too cold to leave them outside, but they should be okay in here.'

Kay dumped her handbag on the draining board, and ran the cold tap until the bowl was three quarters full, wondering what he'd brought home.

As one of the town's more prominent veterinary surgeons, Adam had a habit of bringing his work home with him – literally. She'd had a few months' respite since they'd last played host to one of his patients – a Great Dane who whelped a healthy litter of puppies in the same space the hutch now took up. The worst guest had been a snake that had escaped, and which had achieved legendary status amongst Adam's colleagues.

It hadn't been offered a repeat visit.

She crouched down next to Adam as he lifted a hatch built into the wire mesh section of the hutch and took the bowl from her before placing it in the far corner away from them.

He added the second bowl, into which he had tipped a mixture of seeds and grain.

Kay rested on her haunches, and waited.

'I think they're still getting used to the new surroundings,' said Adam. 'They're quite friendly, once they get used to you. '

Kay opened her mouth to ask him who "they" were, but fell silent when a nose appeared from the enclosed section of the hutch and sniffed the air.

A sandy coloured guinea pig then bustled from the gloom and made its way across the newspaper towards the water bowl, quickly followed by a black and white smaller guinea pig that hovered around its companion before sniffing at the food.

'What are they called?'

'Bonnie and Clyde,' said Adam and walked over to the refrigerator before pulling out a half full bottle of Sauvignon Blanc.

Kay snorted, then stood up as Adam wandered back to her and handed her a wineglass. 'How come they're here?'

Adam used his wineglass to point at the bigger of the two cavies, the sandy coloured one. 'Clyde's got a skin infection, and it can be contagious so the family didn't want their other guinea pigs to catch it. They've got eight in total. Bonnie's always shared a hutch with him, so we're keeping her in for observation for a few days, just in case. Clyde's got some ointment that'll need applying twice a day, but I figured as they fit the remit of "cute and fluffy", you wouldn't mind looking after them while I'm away? The clinic's packed – no room at the inn for them, I'm afraid.'

'That's fine – it'll be nice to have some company while you're gone. At least they won't steal the television remote when I'm not looking.'

He rolled his eyes. 'I have no doubt that, by the time I'm out that front door, you'll have them both on the sofa with you every night. Don't spoil them, all right? They're on a special diet.'

She stuck her tongue out at him then ducked out of the way as he tried to grab her arm, laughing. 'I'm going to get changed. I'll be back down in a minute.'

'I was going to do something simple like pasta tonight – suit you?'

'Fantastic, thanks.'

She put down her wineglass before picking up her handbag and making her way out of the kitchen and up the stairs to the master bedroom at the back of the house.

Below, she could hear the deep tones of Adam's voice as he tried to coax the guinea pigs to eat some food, and smiled as she changed into jeans and a sweatshirt and sorted out a load of laundry.

He was right – she'd enjoy looking after the furry creatures while he was away.

He'd been looking forward to the conference in Aberdeen since booking his ticket nearly five months ago; the event would give him the chance to mingle with his peers, something he rarely had the chance to do outside of his usual circle of contacts and she knew he was keen to soak up the knowledge he'd be surrounded by. The fact that the event included a weekend as well meant there would be plenty of opportunities to network over informal meetings rather than amongst the throng of the scheduled seminars.

Gathering up the pile of dark clothing she'd sorted, she went back down to the kitchen and loaded the washing machine before picking up her wineglass once more, the aroma of garlic and onion heating in a pan filling the air.

While Adam busied himself preparing their dinner, she crouched down to the hutch once more and wiggled her finger through the mesh.

The smaller of the two guinea pigs, Bonnie, pattered across the newspaper and touched her nose to Kay's finger, before turning back to the food.

'They're cute.'

'I knew you'd like them.' Adam took a sip of pasta sauce from a wooden spoon, then added more salt and began to stir once more. 'If you give them a handful of that special food before you go to work in the mornings, they'll be fine all day as long as they've got plenty of water. They can have any vegetable scraps as well. I grabbed a stack of newspapers from the clinic, so you shouldn't run out.' He pointed at the pile of papers he'd left on the worktop nearest the back door, then winked. 'Just remember we have to give them back.'

Kay laughed. 'I know. Don't worry – I've got my hands full at work at the moment. I don't have time for a full-time pet.'

Adam raised an eyebrow, and she proceeded to tell him what she could about her late-night excursion to the M20 and her early start that morning.

'And no-one knows who she is?'

Kay shook her head as she watched him serve their dinner. 'No. I'll find out though. I'll find out why he did this to her.'

'You usually do.'

# CHAPTER SIX

Due to the residents' vehicles already lining the narrow street of terraced houses, Kay ended up parking the pool car a quarter of a mile away from where the incident van had been set up the next morning.

She and Carys elected to take a roundabout route back to where teams of uniformed officers were going from house to house, trying to locate the exact address for the injured driver. They were already hearing feedback over the radio that the neighbours appeared to keep to themselves and, so far, there had been no news they could act upon.

A chill breeze buffeted Kay's hair as they turned the corner into the street where the vehicle had been last seen on CCTV, and she bowed her head against the onslaught.

'Bloody road's designed like a wind tunnel,' said Carys, buttoning her jacket.

Kay murmured her agreement, but her attention was taken by the houses to either side of where they walked.

In front of most, a shallow paved area split the property from the pavement they walked. Some had been enclosed with a low brick wall or hedge to give the residents a modicum of privacy from the street and had been decorated with small collections of potted plants. Others lay bare, exposing cracked concrete and weeds that seemed to dominate the footpath to the houses' front doors.

She craned her neck to see to the end of the road.

The camera that had recorded the car's passing was placed on the side of a corner shop, below an advertising board that stated the first floor was available to lease.

Two uniformed officers exited one of the properties a little ahead of her and Carys and waited by a thin privet hedge to let them pass. Kay recognised one of them as a young probationer she'd worked with six months previously.

He'd already aged with the job, and no longer looked like the scrawny teenager she'd met before.

'Constable Parker, isn't it?'

He nodded.

'Any luck?'

'No. We're only about halfway along, though.'

'Spoken to the shopkeeper?'

'Last on the list for this street, so no – not yet.'

'All right. We'll have a word with him. We're heading that way anyway.'

'Thanks, Sarge.'

'I would've thought they'd have started with the shopkeeper first,' said Carys as they continued past the houses.

'He doesn't own the CCTV camera – it was installed by the council,' said Kay. 'I expect their supervisor's taking the view that we need to find the vehicle owner's house first. Makes sense.'

They passed a female uniformed officer who was pacing the street, collecting the door-to-door enquiry forms from her colleagues as they worked, ready to enter the details into HOLMES on their return to the station.

Kay had sensed the frustration of the uniformed team when chatting with Parker – whoever the driver was, he'd taken care to shield his face from the CCTV cameras his vehicle passed under the night before. The medical staff at the hospital had been adamant the police couldn't take photographs of the man while he was still under observation in the critical care unit – too much risk of infection, Sharp had been told.

It didn't matter – the man's face was so swollen and bruised from the accident and subsequent surgery, it was unlikely anyone would recognise him if they had managed to obtain photographs.

Kay led Carys across the junction at the end of the road and strode across the chewing gum-stained pavement outside the shop.

A group of three teenagers, all on bicycles, glared at her as she approached. The middle-sized one, his hair the colour of washed out bleach, yelled after an older woman who hurried away from the shop tugging a shopping trolley after her.

They fell silent when Kay drew near.

'Do you live around here?'

'Nah,' said the shortest of the three. 'Cheaper ciggies here, innit?'

'Shouldn't you be in school?'

The three lads sniggered.

'Day off,' said the oldest. 'School closed 'cause of a teachers' strike.'

'Got your cigarettes?'

'Yeah.'

'All right. Now, clear off. No hanging around and intimidating the other customers.'

They glared at her, but turned their bikes and pedalled away, catcalling over their shoulders.

Kay shook her head.

'Do you know them?' asked Carys.

'I arrested the oldest one for stealing from a shop over at Shepway eighteen months ago,' said Kay. She sighed. 'No doubt I'll be seeing him again soon.'

She pushed the door to the shop open, an electronic *ping* sounding behind the counter to the left of her.

An elderly man fussed behind it, restacking newspapers and straightening a small display of sweets to the right of the till.

'They're nothing but trouble,' he grumbled. 'You lot should come around more often.'

Kay held out her warrant card. 'DS Hunter, and this

is my colleague, DC Miles. We wanted to ask you a few questions regarding a vehicle spotted on the CCTV camera above the shop.'

'It's not my camera.'

'We're aware of that, thanks – it belongs to the council, right?'

'That's right. Landlord insisted on putting it up there.' He winked. 'Reckon they paid him for the rent of the space. Hate to think what he charged them. That's why the offices above are empty. Costs too much, see?'

Kay turned to a new page of her notebook. 'What's your name, please?'

'Higgins. Malcolm Higgins.'

'And you've had this shop for how long?'

'About twenty years. Should've sold up ages ago. Too late now – business doesn't make enough these days, so no-one's interested in buying it.'

Carys fished out a colour photograph of the vehicle. The image had been captured by one of the CCTV cameras in the town and provided the best view of the car. The one taken from the camera above the shop had been too blurred.

'Have you seen this vehicle around here?'

The man took the photograph from her and peered through smeared glasses at it. His brow puckered.

'I'm not sure,' he said. 'Is he local?'

'That's what we're trying to find out,' said Kay.

'What's he done, then?'

She smiled. 'We wish to speak to him in relation to an ongoing investigation.'

The shopkeeper snorted and passed the photograph back. 'Rehearsed that, did you?'

'Do you know the owner of this vehicle or not?'

He shook his head. 'Can't help you, I'm afraid. I don't really have time to watch the traffic go past.'

Kay glanced over her shoulder at the deserted shop and the dust covering the shelves nearest to her. 'Right. Well, thanks for your time, Mr Higgins.'

She turned back towards the door.

'You make sure you get those coppers out there to come back every day,' the man called after. 'Pain in the arse, those teenage kids.'

The front door burst open and she took a step back in surprise.

Parker entered the shop, slightly out of breath.

'Sarge, we've located the driver's house.'

Kay and Carys hurried after him as he crossed the road, heading towards one of the terrace houses on the opposite side of the street.

'Who confirmed it?' said Kay.

'Elderly couple over at number twenty-two. The husband's confined to a chair most of the day, so they tend to spend their time watching the street,' he said. 'They've seen the car parked outside number twenty-five a few times over the past couple of months.'

'Renting or owners?'

'They say renting – there was a sign put up a while back, and then the bloke moved in. They've seen a woman turn up a few times, but they don't think she lives there. They thought she might have been having an affair with him, because of the way she used to check the street before knocking on the front door. She used to be careful leaving the house, too – the wife says she saw her peering out the front door once or twice before leaving, as if she was afraid of being seen.'

'Interesting. Anyone in now?'

Parker shook his head. 'Place looks empty. No-one answered when we knocked. Thought we'd get you there before we did anything else.'

They stopped on the pavement outside the house, the frontage separated from the street by a wooden fence that held a gate on rusting hinges.

'All right. Let's do this.' Kay pulled out her phone from her bag and dialled Sharp's number. 'Guv? We're going to need that search warrant.'

# CHAPTER SEVEN

Barnes arrived over an hour later, the signed search warrant in his hand.

'Sorry – the magistrate Sharp had briefed was stuck in court, so we had to find another.'

'It happens. Don't worry – I've got officers placed in the road behind this one in case anyone tries to leave over the back fence.'

Ignoring the small group of uniformed officers who had crowded on the pavement beside her, Kay checked the wording of the document, then handed the warrant to the uniformed PC next to her. 'Let's take a look, shall we, Norris?'

'How do you want to do this? Break it down, or pick the lock?'

Kay pivoted and glanced down the street, before turning back to Barnes and Norris. 'We don't have time, and all the neighbours know we're here anyway, so if anyone was going to warn him, they'd have done it by now. Break it down.'

Kay waited while Norris turned to Parker and gestured at the door.

He moved forward, battering ram in his grip, and then aimed it at the door just below the handle, and swung it.

Kay averted her eyes as the door crashed open, sending splinters of wood across the doorstep and over her feet.

'Right, two of you with Barnes, Carys and myself. Everyone else stay outside,' said Kay, slipping gloves over her fingers. 'Let's find out who the hell this bastard is.'

She kicked the bigger splinters out of the way while Norris pushed the door open wide and stepped over the threshold.

'Police!' he called, making his way through the house with Parker at his heels.

Kay hovered at the front door while the two uniformed officers checked downstairs, and caught Norris's eye as he returned from the kitchen shaking his head.

'We'll check upstairs, but you're okay to make a start down here.'

'Thanks. Where's Parker?'

'He went out the back door to check the garden. Don't hold your breath – it doesn't look like it got used much and there's no sign of anyone leaving through the back door before we got here.'

'Okay.' Kay turned to Barnes and Carys. 'Right, let's split up – Carys, you take the kitchen. Barnes and I can split the living room between us.'

'Sarge,' said Carys, and brushed past her, a look of determination on her face.

Kay glanced up the stairs as she led Barnes towards the living room.

Norris stood at the top, and shook his head. 'No-one's around,' he said. 'Do you want me to start the search up here?'

'Go for it.'

As Kay moved into the living room, the first thing she noticed was that the furniture appeared to be a collection of second-hand assortments. Nothing matched.

Everything about the place seemed temporary, as if the tenant didn't expect to return. A two-seater sofa had been placed against the wall behind the door. In front of it, a small table contained an ashtray and a copy of an old newspaper. A small television had been set upon a low chest of drawers in one corner near the window, and what appeared to be a home-made bookshelf leaned precariously against the wall opposite the window.

Kay bent down and began to flick through the pages of the paperbacks. She glanced at Barnes over her shoulder as he pulled open the doors to the chest of drawers and began sorting through it.

'If there was a couple living here, how come it feels like we're only seeing one half?'

She held up one of the books. 'A lot of these are

sport biographies, not the sort of thing I'd expect a woman to read.'

Barnes straightened and placed his hands on his hips as he turned. 'I know what you mean. Even the decor is wrong. I know it's a rental, but you'd expect to see a bit of a personal touch. There's nothing, is there? No photographs, no paperwork lying around—'

'This isn't a home, is it? It's temporary.'

'You think he kept it that way? In case he had to clear out at short notice?'

'That's what I'm thinking. We'll get the place checked out for fingerprints, but given that we know the driver's prints aren't on the system, and nor are his victim's, I don't hold out a lot of hope that we'll find any others. He's been too careful.'

Carys appeared at the doorway. 'There's nothing in the kitchen of interest, either. They certainly don't appear to have cooked at home much. Kitchen bin's been emptied recently – I'll get uniform to take a look in the wheelie bin outside, but the refrigerator's only got the basics in it.'

She fell silent at a call from upstairs.

'Sarge? You need to see this.'

Carys stepped to one side as Kay hurried by her and took the stairs two at a time.

'What is it?'

Norris appeared from a bedroom at the back of the house, his gloved hands clutching a small collection of photographs.

'Found these on top of the wardrobe.'

Kay took the photographs from him and began to flick through the images as Barnes and Carys reached the top of the stairs.

Two of the photographs had been taken in a woodland, the woman relaxed and smiling at the camera as she'd posed beside a large fallen log. In others, the camera had been held aloft and captured the driver and the woman smiling up at the lens.

'Why hide them on top of the wardrobe?' said Barnes, taking the photographs from Kay and holding them so Carys could see at the same time.

'More to the point, those have been taken on an instant camera,' said Kay. 'Why not use his phone?'

'Maybe she's not his wife,' said Norris. 'They could have been having an affair.'

'Good point,' said Kay. 'That'd certainly make sense. Especially with the neighbours telling us how furtive the woman was when she arrived or left the house.'

'If they were having an affair, that also explains why there's nothing here to suggest a woman was living here,' said Carys. 'Maybe he killed her because she was threatening to expose the affair to someone.'

Kay frowned. 'Hang on. Give those back to me a minute.'

She flipped through the images until she found one that included the man and held it up to them. 'I recognise him. I've seen this face before.'

'Where?' said Barnes.

'When the case against Jozef Demiri fell apart and we had to let him go. He arranged for a car to collect him. This guy was his driver.'

# CHAPTER EIGHT

Kay paced the room and rubbed at her right eye.

Despite the discovery at the house in Tonbridge, she couldn't abandon the search process and had to wait until Harriet and her team had turned up so she could brief them.

Instead, she had sent Barnes and Carys back to the incident room to report their findings to the rest of the team and start the process of checking tenancy records for the property and find any other online photographs that matched the image of the man they'd discovered at the house.

On her return to Maidstone, she'd been disappointed to discover that they had found nothing, and that Sharp had been called to a meeting at headquarters on the other side of the town and wouldn't be back until the afternoon briefing.

She wanted to talk through her theory with him, determined to prove there was a connection between the driver and Jozef Demiri, an Albanian who was known to run one of the more lucrative organised crime syndicates in the south-east, but who had managed to avoid any criminal charges – despite their best efforts.

Undeterred by Sharp's absence, she had tasked the team to spend the rest of the day making phone calls and checking the information they had to date to try to get a breakthrough.

Three hours later, and she was wondering if Demiri would evade them once more when a loud whoop reached her ears.

Gavin tossed his mobile phone onto his desk and spun his chair round to face her.

'That was Charlie – he's helping Harriet with the forensics of the vehicle in the accident.'

'Yeah, I remember him from the other night,' said Kay. 'What's he got?'

Gavin grinned and held up his notebook. 'Partial Vehicle Identification Number off the chassis. He says most of it had been filed off, but once they'd removed all the mud and grime, they managed to get something for us. And – get this – it's different to the one on the registration certificate linked to the licence plate.'

'Put it in the system,' said Kay, and scooted her chair across to Gavin's desk.

He turned and opened up a new window on his computer, typed in the details and pressed "Enter".

Kay sipped from a mug of tepid tea while they waited.

Once, soon after passing his exams, Gavin had

mentioned to her that he'd been surprised at how ponderous murder investigations could be.

Kay had smiled, and explained it was often the smallest details that led to the biggest breakthroughs, and she'd noticed since then that the recently qualified detective had been one of the few content to spend hours trawling through minute information in the hope of a breakthrough. It often worked, or at least provided the team with solid data they could follow up on with great effect.

'Here you go,' he said, and pointed at the screen. His brow creased. 'Hang on. It's registered to a business.'

'Which one?' Kay bent over and scanned the lines of text displayed across the screen.

'Delight Investments.'

'What?' Kay straightened and twisted round to summon Barnes, but he'd already pushed himself out of his chair and was moving towards them.

'Delight Investments,' repeated Gavin. His eyes shifted between Kay and Barnes. 'Why? Is there a problem? Who owns the company?'

Kay swallowed, fighting to keep her excitement in check.

'Jozef Demiri,' she said. 'Josef bloody Demiri. I *knew* it.'

She straightened as Sharp pushed through the door and strode across the room to where she stood, and their eyes locked.

'Why am I hearing Demiri's name?'

Kay quickly updated him about the search at the property, and then pointed at Gavin's computer.

'He's connected, guv. I recognised the driver, and the car's registered to Demiri's business. We're onto something here.'

In reply, he held up his hand. 'All right, you've got me convinced. I'll make some phone calls – DCI Larch will have to be brought up to speed, so I'll need you to put together a summary report for me about this investigation to date before you leave today in order that we can get extra resources. You know what to do.'

'Guv.'

'Carys – while that's happening, can you and Gavin pull together everything on our system about Demiri's business assets, including Delight Investments – find out what else he's got listed under that name and others together with any knowledge we have about people working for him. Tread carefully. We know what he's capable of,' he said, aiming an apologetic glance at Kay, 'and none of us want a repeat of last year's events.'

'Will do,' said Carys.

'Finally, security,' said Sharp, and waited until he had everyone's attention. 'Based on what happened last time, and so no-one has to go through what Kay did with the Professional Standards investigation, this incident room will now be locked down. No-one will take work home with them. The room will be opened by me at seven o'clock in the morning, and I'll be locking it at seven o'clock every night. All evidence will be logged by Debbie, who reports directly to me. You want something out of evidence to review, you see me first, got it?'

A murmur of agreement swept through the room.

'We *are* going to get this bastard,' said Sharp. 'But he's cunning, and dangerous. If anyone has reason to believe that they are in danger, or you are threatened by anyone in any way, you come to see me immediately. Is that understood?'

'Guv.'

Sharp turned back to Kay. 'We tread carefully. We've got one shot at this.'

She nodded, fighting down the adrenalin that had started to course through her veins.

'Don't worry, guv. We'll do this properly. I want Demiri put away – for a long time.'

# CHAPTER NINE

Kay pulled her car out of the police station car park, indicated right and merged into the remains of the late afternoon commuting traffic.

As she turned left and drove past the large multi-storey car park and adjoining supermarket, her mind returned to Jozef Demiri.

He had been almost within her clutches once, nearly two years ago.

She and her colleagues had gathered enough evidence to support an investigation into Demiri's business dealings, and everything pointed to him running an extensive drugs operation between the Continent and his base in the south-east corner of England.

However, while a surveillance team was waiting for Demiri's return from the Continent, a gun seized from a routine traffic stop and which they all thought had

Demiri's fingerprints on it went missing from the evidence locker at the police station.

The aftermath had been shocking, starting with a Professional Standards investigation that accused Kay of taking the weapon.

It had devastating consequences on her health. She had miscarried the baby girl she had only found out weeks before she was carrying and despite her best efforts, her career had never fully recovered.

She'd vowed revenge on Demiri ever since.

She fought down her excitement as she turned into the lane that led to her house, and twisted her hand on the steering wheel to check her watch.

Adam had left the house early that morning, keen to get to the clinic to catch up on paperwork before the morning's appointments began to filter through the doors, and she hoped he'd be home at a reasonable time.

They had another day together before he flew to Aberdeen for his conference, and she wanted to make the most of her time with him.

As the car passed their local pub, a smile formed on her lips.

Pulling into the driveway of the house she locked her car and hurried to the front door.

'I'm home!'

'Upstairs.'

Kay bounded up the stairs and into their bedroom at the front of the house. 'The pub looks quiet – fancy a drink?'

Adam appeared from the en suite bathroom,

towelling his hair. He grinned. 'Sounds like a great idea.'

'Good – I'll get changed and we'll go straight away.'

Twenty minutes later they had grabbed a small table in the corner of the public bar at the front of the pub, each with a pint of real ale in front of them.

'Cheers,' said Adam, clinking his glass against hers before taking a long sip. 'Oh, I needed that.'

Kay savoured the beer, licked a trace of froth off her lips and sank back into the soft leather of her chair. She craned her neck to look through the bar to the lounge area, but only two people sat on bar stools chatting to the landlady.

The rest of the pub was deserted; the regular evening crowd would be in later.

Kay relaxed. The only problem with being a police officer in a town rather than a large city, was that sometimes she'd see someone she'd arrested in the past walk through the door of a pub or pass her in the supermarket.

She'd given up diving behind displays of soup tins or the latest book offerings years ago and instead glared back at the offenders, but it was still a welcome relief to find none of her past encounters from successful arrests yet drank in her local pub.

She pushed her hair behind her ear and took another sip of her beer.

'I might have to stay in Aberdeen a bit longer,' said Adam, his voice breaking into her thoughts.

'Problem?'

'No – one of the other guys going to the conference has a practice specialising in the horse racing industry. I wouldn't mind spending some time with him while I'm there, that's all. Okay with you?'

'Of course.' She smiled. 'It'd be a great opportunity for you.'

Adam's busy clinic was popular with the local community, and he was one of the few local vets experienced with racehorses and their foibles.

He placed his half-empty pint glass on a cardboard coaster and reached out for her hand. 'I'm thinking of expanding the business. Taking on someone else to deal with the small stuff so I can concentrate on networking more. There are some speaking opportunities on the Continent I'd like to explore.'

'Wow.' Kay twisted in her seat to face him.

A hopeful expression crossed his features.

She knew how good he was at his work; until a few years ago he'd been a regular contributor to veterinary journals and had participated in conferences up and down the country. Then, the business had taken off and he'd put all his energy into establishing and growing that.

'You're good at sharing what you know,' she said, squeezing his hand. 'I think that's a great idea – as long as you don't stretch yourself too thin. You don't want to get exhausted from it all.'

'Don't worry, I'll only do a few a year to keep my hand in. We could travel together, if your work allowed it. About time we had a holiday anyway. We could turn it into a working holiday – I could do my lecture, and then we could have a few days to explore before we come home.'

'Sounds great. I could get used to that.'

'Fantastic.' He smiled, and took a long draught of his beer, a look of contentment in his eyes. 'So, are you going to tell me what's happening about that car crash the other night? Any developments?'

Kay checked the landlord was still busy with customers in the other bar, and lowered her voice to tell Adam what she could of the ongoing investigation.

'The thing is,' she said, and took a deep breath. 'Gavin traced the vehicle identification number to a business owned by Jozef Demiri.'

Adam's eyes hardened and he set down his glass. 'Demiri?'

Kay put her finger to her lips. 'Yeah.'

'Kay, listen to me. You stay away from him, all right? I know it's your job, but let one of the others deal with him. It's too dangerous.'

'I need to do this, Adam. I want him put away, and I want to be there when we do it.'

'You know how dangerous he is. I know you want this, but for Christ's sake don't go anywhere near him on your own.'

'I won't be on my own. Sharp'll be with me.' Her mouth quirked. 'I don't think he trusts me with what I'll do to Demiri if he lets me go alone.'

'It's not funny, Kay. Not with his reputation.'

She held up her hand. 'I know. I'm sorry. I'll be careful.'

'I wish I wasn't going away now.'

'I'll be fine. Honest.'

He ran a hand over his face. 'You make sure you lock all the doors and windows while I'm away. And keep the security lights on around the house, too.'

'Okay.'

'Promise me, Kay.'

'I promise.'

'All right.' His eyes softened and he pointed at her empty glass. 'Another one of those?'

'Thought you'd never ask.'

# CHAPTER TEN

Kay and Sharp left the police station immediately after the next morning's briefing, intent on interviewing Jozef Demiri as soon as possible.

Kay drove, their pace slowed by the amount of traffic on the A20 between Maidstone and Ashford – a result of a multiple collision at Folkestone, and the authorities' decision to utilise the M20 motorway for Operation Stack, a strategy whereby all the trucks that couldn't use the Channel Tunnel or ferries to France were parked on the motorway, thereby preventing anyone else from using it.

'Just as well we didn't make an appointment,' said Sharp, grumbling under his breath.

Kay said nothing, the traffic jam doing nothing to tame her excitement at the prospect of meeting Demiri face to face.

Proving who was responsible for removing the gun from the evidence locker and bringing Demiri to justice was all that had kept her focused during her darkest moments.

She slowed as they entered the outskirts of Ashford and negotiated a series of roundabouts before she swung the car into a small business park.

Signs stacked one on top of the other like a totem pole at the entrance to the business park confirmed the presence of Demiri's offices. It didn't take long to find the glass-enshrouded low level unit that his software business occupied. She locked the car and they made their way towards the building, Sharp at her side.

'I'll take the lead,' he said. 'We both know we're going to be under the microscope with this one. I don't want to give Larch or anyone else an excuse to question this investigation.'

'Understood, guv.'

Kay fought down her excitement and followed Sharp as he approached the double doors to the building. Her eyes fell upon a brass plaque to the side of the entrance portico.

*Delight Investments.*

She had been amazed DCI Larch hadn't intervened in their plans to speak with Demiri. As it was, after delivering the report Kay had prepared for him, Sharp had had to clear the meeting with the Chief Superintendent, and was ordered to report to headquarters the moment they returned from their interview.

An intercom was set underneath the plaque, and she

waited while Sharp pressed the button and announced their arrival.

A faint *buzz* sounded, followed by a *click*, and the door opened under Sharp's touch.

The door closed automatically behind Kay, and the thick carpet under her feet silenced her footsteps as they approached a sumptuous mahogany reception desk. A chandelier hung from the high ceiling, and Kay realised with a shock that it was real crystal. It seemed out of place within a modern office building, and she couldn't help but wonder who Demiri was trying to impress.

A young woman sat behind the reception desk, her blonde hair swept up into an efficient bun, and Kay realised the woman's black suit probably cost three times as much as the one she herself wore. The woman looked up from her computer screen as they approached and smiled.

'Good morning. Can I help you?'

Kay thought she could hear the trace of a foreign accent, but the woman's English was perfectly enunciated.

'Detective Inspector Sharp, and my colleague Detective Sergeant Hunter,' said Sharp by way of introduction. He held up his warrant card. 'We'd like a word with Mr Demiri, please.'

'Do you have an appointment?'

'No. This isn't a social visit.'

'Oh.' The woman's face fell, her smile disappearing, and she glanced back at the computer screen. 'Well, I'm afraid he has an appointment in half an hour, and his calendar is busy for the rest of the day.'

'We'll see him now, if you could let him know we're here.'

The woman bit her lip. 'That – that's rather awkward.'

Sharp smiled. 'I understand. We can wait here until he's finished his other appointments, if you like?'

A look of horror spread across the woman's face, and Kay couldn't help but feel sorry for her.

Evidently the thought of two plainclothes police detectives sitting in her boss's plush reception area filled her with dread.

Despite knowing Sharp was bluffing, Kay relished the thought of sitting in Demiri's office all day so she could find out who his other appointments were with. It would surely make for interesting updates to the HOLMES2 database.

'Wait here,' said the receptionist, rising from her chair. 'I'll be right back.'

'Thanks.'

Sharp turned away from the desk and winked at Kay.

'Don't look too happy,' he murmured. 'There's a camera up in the corner to your six o'clock position.'

Kay brought her fist to her mouth, and cleared her throat. 'Seems quite fond of those.'

'Steady.'

She'd never told anyone about the cameras she'd found hidden in her house a few months ago, no-one except Sharp who, with his ex-military background, had somehow managed to have the devices removed without alerting the perpetrators to the fact they'd been found. The equipment had simply ceased to work one day. Kay suspected Demiri was responsible, but she had no proof and given her workload over the months since, she hadn't had a chance to investigate further.

Not that she'd tell Sharp if she had.

They both turned at the sound of a door opening to their left, and the receptionist reappeared, closely followed by a man in his late fifties.

Kay took a step back, her heart ratcheting up a notch.

Jozef Demiri exuded evil, as far as she was concerned.

His bulk ensured he dominated the space, his deep brown hooded eyes boring into hers as he strode towards them. Immaculately dressed in a black suit that accentuated his collar-length white hair, he let his tanned skin crease as his brow furrowed.

'Detective Hunter. I'm surprised to see you here.'

'Mr Demiri, we have some preliminary questions we'd like to ask you in relation to an ongoing enquiry,' said Sharp, not bothering with introductions again. 'Is there somewhere we can talk in private?'

Demiri chuckled, then checked the solid gold watch on his wrist and sighed. 'All right, Detective Sharp. I'll play your games. Beatrice – I'll use the conference room here. Knock on the door five minutes before my next appointment.'

'Yes, Mr Demiri.'

'Shall we?'

He crossed the plush carpet to a panelled door, held it open and gestured to Sharp and Kay to enter.

Kay shivered as she squeezed past him, the warmth from his breath tickling her face as she entered the room.

'I've been waiting for you, Kay,' he murmured.

# CHAPTER ELEVEN

Kay waited until Demiri moved to the head of the oval conference table, grateful that Sharp took a minute to pull out a chair for her well away from where the Albanian sat.

A mixture of excitement and trepidation swept through her.

Professionally, she wanted justice for everything the man had done to her and others, but his comment as they'd entered the room had unnerved her.

As he moved an upside-down water glass away from his elbow, she wondered what he'd meant by his words.

Was he talking about the car crash and subsequent discovery of the woman's body, or something else?

Was he simply trying to gain the upper hand on the interview?

'Mr Demiri, we'll keep this formal,' said Sharp.

Demiri nodded, and leaned on the table, his hands loosely clasped together. 'As you wish.'

His eyes never left Kay's as Sharp read out the formal caution and then opened a plastic folder he'd brought with him and slid a photograph across the table.

Demiri's hand slapped it to a standstill, then spun it around. He glanced up at Sharp. 'Explain.'

'This vehicle was involved in a motor vehicle accident two nights ago on the M20. Tracing the car's movements using CCTV, we've located the property rented by the driver.'

He pushed a copy of one of the photos discovered at the property across the table.

Demiri's face remained impassive.

'Does this person look familiar to you?'

'No. Should he?'

'The thing is, this man is a known associate of yours, Mr Demiri,' said Kay. 'He drives for you.'

Demiri's eyes sparkled as he leaned forward, and then he shrugged. 'No. I do not know him. You must remember, Detective Hunter, I am a busy man. I have many people who may have worked for me at one time or another. I cannot recall all of them.'

'Mr Demiri, do you recognise the woman in the photograph?'

'No.'

'If you could take another look at the photograph, please.'

Demiri sighed, and took the photograph Kay shoved across to him. He glanced at it, then passed it back with the others. 'I don't know her. What's she got to do with him and a car accident?'

'Her body was found in the boot of the car,' said Sharp.

'Maybe it was a domestic argument gone wrong, you think?'

'It's one of the avenues of enquiry we're pursuing, yes.'

Kay slipped the photographs across the desk to Sharp and watched as he extracted a further image from the folder.

'This is a photograph taken at the scene of the accident,' said Sharp. 'Having checked with the licensing authorities, it seems the car belongs to you. If this man was no longer driving for you, can you explain why he was in your car two nights ago?'

'I've no idea, really. Perhaps he was running an errand for one of my members of staff.'

'Wouldn't you have told them he no longer worked for you?'

'It must've slipped their minds.'

'Mr Demiri, where were you two nights ago between eight o'clock and midnight?'

Demiri beamed. 'I was at the launch of a new business venture of mine; an exclusive club in Romford. Many guests. Many *witnesses*,' he added, glaring at the senior detective. He turned his attention to Kay, a smile playing on his lips. 'Maybe you could join us for the opening night next month, Detective Hunter? It would be a pleasure to see you again.'

Kay lowered her gaze and cursed at the shiver that wracked her shoulders.

*He knows*, she thought. *He knows I found the cameras and microphones.*

A low chuckle emanated from the end of the table, and she jerked her head up to see Demiri watching her, a predatory smile on his lips.

Sharp cleared his throat. 'I don't think DS Hunter would wish to socialise with you, in all honesty. We'd like to make arrangements to interview the rest of your staff here—'

'Impossible.'

'I don't think you fully appreciate your tenuous position, Mr Demiri. As I said, we'll be making arrangements to interview your staff here, as well as anyone else associated with you during the course of our enquiries.'

Demiri held up his hand to stop Sharp, and glanced beyond Kay's position at a knock on the door, a moment before it opened.

'Mr Demiri, you requested a five minute warning.'

'Thank you, Beatrice.'

Demiri rose from his chair, buttoned his jacket and gestured towards the door.

'Now, Detectives, if you please – I have an important meeting to attend to, and you've already taken up enough of my time this morning.'

Sharp handed the man one of his business cards. 'We'll be in touch.'

'I'm sure you will,' said Demiri and walked them to the door.

Kay stopped on the threshold and turned to him.

'Who drives for you now?'

Demiri held up his hands. 'I like to drive myself these days.'

'Good drivers hard to find?'

'*Trustworthy* drivers are hard to find, Detective Hunter.'

# CHAPTER TWELVE

Jozef Demiri pressed a button on the remote control, then flung the device onto the polished surface of the conference table where it skidded to a halt next to an empty crystal water jug.

The screen on the wall sprang to life; a set of nine images from inside the building and out.

He moved closer and folded his arms as he watched the detective and her superior pause in the car park a few metres from where they'd left his offices. Detective Hunter stared up at the CCTV camera fixed to the gables before turning back to Sharp.

Demiri exhaled.

After all this time, after all the effort that had gone into ensuring she dropped the case against him, it seemed they would have their time after all.

A smile played on his lips, before he loosened his tie and undid the top button of his shirt.

His receptionist had lied, of course.

He had no appointments for the rest of the day. All of his business was conducted at night, after hours, under cover of darkness.

However, the office at the business park served to keep up appearances and lent some weight to the persona he had been careful to build.

That of a respectable, hardworking businessman.

At least the hardworking part was right, he mused.

Ever since he'd arrived in the county twenty years ago, he'd been focused solely on creating and maintaining a business empire that now stretched beyond the south-east coast of England.

His network of contacts and connections spread like tendrils throughout the southern counties and into northern France, and his reputation for brutality ensured few dared to cross his path.

He adjusted the gold cuff links at his wrists, before turning his back on the screens and pressing a button on the console at the head of the table.

'Beatrice, send in Oliver Tavender.'

'Right away, Mr Demiri.'

Demiri smiled. The young woman that sat outside in the reception area had been hand-picked by him, saving her from a future that had befallen many of her Romanian compatriots.

He knew he could trust her – and she knew he was well aware of her family's whereabouts in Brasov should she dare cross him.

Her loyalty was assured.

There was a knock on the door two minutes later,

and a burly man in his late thirties entered the meeting room, his thin hair slicked back giving him an aged appearance. A little taller than Demiri, he was as wide with pockmarked skin across his nose, which looked as if it had been broken more than once.

He shut the door and remained standing at the foot of the long table, his hands crossed in front of him, his pale blue eyes unblinking.

'I've had a visit from Detective Hunter and her boss,' said Demiri, his voice level.

'I saw, on the cameras. Do they suspect anything?'

A thin smile crossed Demiri's lips. 'Oh, they always suspect something,' he said. 'It's simply a matter of *what* they suspect.'

'Stokes?'

'Crashed his car on the motorway after leaving here.'

'Did he survive?'

'My contacts tell me he has.'

'A pity.'

'Indeed. Although it's early days – apparently, the surgery was touch and go, and he's still in intensive care.'

'I can't get to him there.'

'I wasn't going to suggest you do. There are other ways.'

'What about the dead girl?'

Demiri shrugged. 'Not our problem.' He pointed at the screen. 'She, however, *is*.'

Tavender moved closer and peered at the image.

Hunter and the senior detective appeared deep in conversation, their heads bowed as they walked towards their vehicle.

Demiri drummed his fingers on the table. 'It is unfortunate we haven't been able to watch her more closely.'

'The listening devices were of the highest quality,' said Tavender. 'As were the cameras we installed in her house.'

'They should not have failed.'

'I'm sorry, Mr Demiri – it happens—'

Demiri waved away the excuse and glared at the retreating figures on the screen, before leaning forward and pressing a different button. The screen flickered, and then switched to a different channel. 'Forget it. It is too late now.'

'What do you want us to do, Mr Demiri?'

'Keep an eye on her. Keep it low-key for the moment. When the time comes, I'll tell you. Detective Sergeant Kay Hunter is going to wish she'd never met me.' He swivelled his chair round until he could watch the show being broadcast on the screen to his side.

'Your obsession with her will be the death of you, Jozef,' said Tavender softly.

Demiri chuckled. 'Or her.'

# CHAPTER THIRTEEN

Sharp stood aside and held the door to the incident room open for Kay.

'Get the team rounded up. We'll debrief early today. I'm sure they're keen to know how it went before I head over to headquarters.'

'Guv.'

'How'd you get on?' said Barnes as she dumped her bag on her chair and signalled to him to move towards the whiteboard at the end of the room.

'He's stalling,' she murmured. 'Said he doesn't know who the man is – or, at least, he can't remember his name. Says he doesn't know who the woman is, either.'

'Is he telling the truth, do you think?'

'No. I reckon he's lying through his teeth. He was too smooth, Ian. Ready for us.'

They broke off their conversation as Gavin wheeled

his chair towards the whiteboard and sat down, his excitement palpable.

Kay moved closer to the front of the room, her thoughts tumbling over each other.

She couldn't help feeling that they'd missed something, that she should've left Demiri's offices victorious. Instead, it seemed she'd miscalculated what his response to their unannounced visit would be, and it left her worried.

'Okay, Sarge?'

She turned to Gavin, forcing a smile. 'Yes, thanks. Lots to think about, that's all.'

'We'll get him, don't you worry.'

'You betcha.'

Kay watched as Carys approached Sharp, and he stooped a little so he could listen to what the young detective constable had to say, and then gestured to the waiting group.

She joined Kay and Barnes and pulled a chair out next to them.

'News?' said Kay.

'Yes. Sharp's asked me to hang fire, and we'll go through it with everyone.'

Kay nodded, and settled in for the debrief.

It made sense to wait for Carys's news if it was going to involve the whole team, rather than have her repeat it – the group discussion often unearthed new ideas and theories, which would otherwise be lost.

Sharp began the briefing, noting the date and time

for the official record, and provided the team with a detailed account of the interview with Jozef Demiri.

Despite being present at the time, Kay took notes alongside her colleagues, knowing from experience that often someone else's viewpoint could be different from her own and provide insights that she might not otherwise have considered.

'Where are we up to with the post mortem on the female victim?' said Sharp, casting his eyes around the room for an answer.

Gavin raised his pen in the air. 'Lucas says it'll be tomorrow morning now, guv. Bit of a backlog, he says. Something to do with being understaffed.'

Sharp sighed. 'Nothing changes, does it?'

No-one answered; the question was rhetorical and everyone knew how busy the small mortuary at the hospital in Dartford was, particularly with the onset of the colder months.

'Any more news from Maidstone Hospital, guv?' said Gavin.

'The driver underwent further surgery this morning to pin his broken leg,' said Sharp. 'It'll be a couple of days before we can question him. This'd be a good time for you to bring everyone up to speed on what we have from Harriet's team please, Carys.'

Miles cleared her throat and rose from her seat, before standing next to Sharp. She flipped open her notebook, read a couple of lines, then raised her gaze to the waiting team.

'Right, well first of all, there's no record of the

driver's fingerprints being on any of the databases. Me and Gavin spent the day going through HOLMES2, and we widened our search countrywide as well – he doesn't exist.'

'Unusual for someone in his position to have no prior conviction or arrest,' said Kay.

'Maybe that's what made him an attractive employment prospect for Demiri?' said Barnes.

A murmur of agreement passed through the room.

'Speaking of the driver, I'm going to arrange to have the security on his room increased immediately,' said Sharp. 'I'm sure our visit to Demiri will have rattled him, despite his attempts to remain cool. The last thing we want is for him to arrange for an unfortunate accident to happen to his ex-driver before we've had a chance to speak to him.'

He gestured to Carys to continue.

'We also have no record for the female victim. Again, none of the fingerprints taken from her by Lucas, the pathologist, or Harriet's team were matched by our databases, but we'll keep digging.'

Kay could sense the frustration amongst the small group. The thought that they had Demiri in their sights, but no evidence with which to charge him was already starting to rankle.

'Harriet did come up with something for us though,' said Carys.

'Hallelujah,' murmured Barnes, and then held up his hand in apology as she lowered her notebook and glared at him.

'Two sets of prints were taken from the steering wheel, handbrake and door handles that match a couple of blokes that have prior convictions for burglary offences. Gary Hudson and John Millard.'

'Do we have any idea where they are now?' said Gavin.

Barnes checked his watch. 'It's four o'clock. Knowing those two, we'll find them in the pub on Union Street.'

# CHAPTER FOURTEEN

Despite Carys and Gavin's frustration, Sharp elected to let Kay and Barnes interview the two men once they'd been brought in for questioning.

'You two aren't known to Demiri,' he'd said by way of explanation, and within the confines of his office. 'I'd like to keep it that way. You've seen what he's capable of doing, and the reach he has. You've seen what happened to Kay. I'd rather keep you at arm's length from this until it's absolutely necessary.'

The two detective constables had murmured their assent before Sharp had dismissed them, but Kay could sense their disappointment as they left the room, and turned to the DI once the door had closed.

'Don't leave them too far out of the loop, guv,' she said. 'I wouldn't want them getting frustrated and then deciding to go off and try to solve this themselves.'

'Point taken,' said Sharp.

The three of them had then spent another twenty

minutes discussing interview tactics before Kay and Barnes had made their way to the interview rooms.

'Rock, paper, scissors,' murmured Barnes.

Kay held up her fist.

'Goon one it is then,' he grinned, and pushed the interview room door open.

Duty solicitors had been assigned to each of the men, and now as Kay entered the room, the one that had been assigned to Gary Hudson rose from his chair and adjusted his tie as he stood.

'My client denies all charges.'

'Whoa,' said Kay, and waved him back into his seat. 'Settle down, we haven't got that far yet.'

She avoided Barnes's eyes, knowing he was itching to aim a witty retort at the eager young criminal solicitor, and instead reached over to begin the recording.

She formally cautioned the man sat in front of her, waited while Barnes settled into his seat, and then opened a folder and slid a photograph of the crashed vehicle across the table.

'Right, Mr Hudson. This car was involved in an accident two nights ago on the M20 near Harrietsham. The driver is currently in hospital, and the body of this woman—,' she said, pausing to slide another photograph across the table, '—was found in the boot of the car. Dead. Now, perhaps you could explain to me why we found your fingerprints on the vehicle.'

The young solicitor paled at the sight of the woman's body.

Patrick, the CSI photographer, had taken a number of images from the scene of the accident, and Barnes had chosen the most shocking one he could find, in the hope it would elicit a response from the known criminal.

Hudson leaned forward, his hands in his pockets, and peered at the two photographs, then shook his head.

'Don't know anything about that.'

'When did you last come into contact with the vehicle?'

Easing back into his seat, Hudson stared at Kay through hooded eyes. 'Can't say I recall.'

'When was the last time you saw the vehicle?'

He shrugged. 'Dunno. Maybe three or four months ago.'

'Who did the vehicle belong to?'

'Not me.'

'That's fine. Who *did* own it?'

Another shrug. 'Not sure. I didn't drive it. I was just a passenger in it a couple of times.'

'A couple of times? Right, and where were you going as a passenger in the vehicle those times?'

'Can't remember.'

'Who was driving?'

'Can't remember.'

Kay narrowed her eyes. 'You might want to work on your recall a bit, Gary. At the present time, we're investigating a murder.' She tapped the photograph of the dead woman. 'With your fingerprints on the vehicle, you're currently a suspect in that murder.'

Hudson shrugged, his expression bored.

'Fine,' said Kay, and stood. 'Interview terminated at five-fifteen. Mr...?'

'Dundas,' said the young solicitor.

'We'll be holding your client in the cells overnight pending further enquiries, Mr Dundas. We'll be in touch when we're ready to speak with him again. You may want to have a quiet word with him about being a bit more forthcoming with his answers, to avoid another conviction being added to his existing tally.'

The solicitor's mouth opened and closed soundlessly as Kay and Barnes left the room.

Reaching the corridor, Kay signalled to the custody sergeant to take Hudson to the cells, and then turned to her colleague.

'Let's hope his friend is a bit more chatty.'

'Let's hope his duty solicitor looks older than twelve.'

'Couldn't fault his enthusiasm, though, could you? I thought he'd lit a rocket under his backside when we walked in.'

Barnes grinned, then straightened his face and pushed open the door to the second interview room.

Kay recognised the older solicitor, nodded to him, then let Barnes begin the recording and cite the relevant caution.

John Millard was another career criminal who they'd arrested time and time again over the years for vehicle theft, drug offences and the like and seemed as unimpressed as Hudson at being interviewed.

As the older detective worked through a similar set

of questions and displayed the photographs from the crash scene in front of the man, Kay checked her notes against what they had learned to date.

'Your fingerprints were found on the steering column of the vehicle, Millard,' said Barnes. 'Now, why would that be?'

Millard was younger than his counterpart, and not as experienced in being questioned by the police. His eyes shifted from left to right, and his Adam's apple bobbed in his throat as his gaze fell to the image of the dead woman once more.

His shoulders hunched over as he moved his arms across his chest, and Kay noticed a slight trembling of his hands.

'John, I know you're scared, but we really need to find out what happened to this woman.'

Millard lifted his gaze to hers, and swallowed. 'He'll kill me.'

'We can do our best to protect you.'

'I-I've got a young family.'

'Tell us what you know, Millard,' said Barnes. 'The quicker we finish this conversation, the quicker we can start the process to ensure their safety.'

'My daughter's only six. Can you *imagine* what he'd do to her?'

He lifted a shaking hand to a scab on his jaw and ran his fingers across it, his eyes returning to the photograph of the dead woman.

Kay leaned forward before he drew blood from the old wound. 'Tell us, John.'

'I – I think I drove it,' he said, dropping his hand into his lap. 'Once or twice.'

'Whose car was it?'

'Not sure. I had to pick it up from a lay-by outside Ashford, on the Tenterden Road. That's all I know. Honest. Keys were hidden in the wheel arch.'

'What did you use the vehicle for?'

'Nothing much.'

'Elaborate, please John,' said Kay.

'That means tell us in more detail,' said Barnes as confusion spread across the man's face.

'This and that. One time, I had to pick up some cheap booze from a supermarket at Calais. That sort of thing. Nothing illegal,' he added, his eyes wide.

Fifteen minutes later, and Kay and Barnes had gleaned no further information from Millard. Like his colleague, he was choosing to remain silent rather than implicate himself or his boss in any investigation.

Frustrated, they ended the interviews, sent the men back to the cells, and trudged back to the incident room.

Debbie handed them both a mug of tea as they took their seats and brought the rest of the team up to date with their findings.

It didn't take long.

'Okay, well Carys had a bit more luck with the vehicle, so we're not done yet,' said Sharp. He tapped his finger on the licence plate in one of the photographs of the crash site pinned to the whiteboard. 'The Driver and Vehicle Licensing Agency have a record of this car being sold three months ago by a garage in a small village outside Hythe, but the buyer's details have been entered incorrectly on the vehicle log book form.'

'Classic,' said Gavin, shaking his head.

A murmur of agreement filled the room.

If a car was disposed of under suspicious circumstances, or the buyer wanted to remain unknown, it was a simple enough exercise to forge documentation or complete required transfer forms in an illegible scrawl.

The Licencing Authority dealt with so many documents on a day-to-day basis that it could be six months before one of their administrative staff found the time to query the discrepancy with the seller of the vehicle.

'Kay, I'd like you and Barnes to go there first thing tomorrow morning. Don't phone ahead – I don't want to give the owner the chance to come up with an excuse.'

'Or an alibi,' said Carys.

# CHAPTER FIFTEEN

Kay turned her key in the lock, stepped into the warmth of the hallway and nearly tripped over the suitcase that had been left open next to the front door.

'Sorry,' Adam called from the kitchen. 'Last minute packing. Nearly forgot spare razors.'

Kay looped her handbag over the newel post of the stair bannister and hooked her jacket over the top of it before kicking off her shoes and padding along the hallway.

Adam stood next to the sink, washing out a coffee mug. He glanced over his shoulder as she appeared.

'I'm wondering whether I should go,' he said, drying his hands on a tea towel.

She frowned. 'Why? What's happened? Is there something wrong at work?'

'No,' he said, and crossed the tiles to where she stood at the centre worktop. He reached up and hooked a tendril of her hair behind her ear. 'I'm worried about you. About this investigation with Demiri.'

'I'll be okay.' She wrapped her fingers around his. 'You can't cancel. You've been looking forward to this conference for months. Think of all the networking opportunities you'll miss out on if you don't go.'

'I know, Kay but there'll be another conference next year.'

She squeezed his hand before moving to one of the bar stools next to the worktop, and sitting. 'Adam, you know as well as I do that if you don't go now, you won't meet the same people that are there this year. You don't have to worry about me – Sharp was with me earlier today when we spoke to Demiri.' Her lips thinned. 'Demiri's a lying bastard, but it went fine. No threats. No bluster. Nothing at all. Besides, I think it'll be weeks before we've got anything to pin on him – he's too clever. There are too many layers to his organisation we have to chip away at first. You'll be back in, what, three days?'

'Yeah.'

'What time's your taxi picking you up?'

Adam checked his watch. 'It'll be here in twenty minutes or so.'

'Go and get those razors, or you'll forget them.'

'Right.'

She waited until he'd left the kitchen before she let out her breath.

She could hear the note of fear in his voice, and knew he was still unsure about leaving her alone in the house now that she and the team were once more going after Demiri, but she couldn't let the Albanian rule their lives.

He'd already caused too much damage, too much grief, but she was determined that he'd pay for what he'd done to her.

She slid off the stool and pulled open one of the cupboard doors, took out a wine glass and then selected one of the bottles of Shiraz off the rack built into the central worktop and poured out a measure.

Adam's footsteps sounded on the stairs and he grinned as he entered the kitchen.

'I reckon I've got time for a small one of those,' he said, grabbing a glass and filling it.

'Cheers,' said Kay. 'Here's to a successful trip, and lots of ideas for the business.'

He clinked his glass against hers. 'Oh, I've got plenty of those,' he said. 'It's the implementation that has my head spinning.'

'Do you have anyone in mind you're going to employ to give you some spare time?'

'There's a young graduate over at a practice near Paddock Wood I've got my eye on. Met him at that function we went to a couple of months ago. I know he's keen to move into a larger surgery environment and take on more responsibility.'

'Sounds good.'

'Yeah. I'll give him a call next week once I'm back.'

The sound of a car pulling onto the driveway

reached them, and Kay craned her neck as headlight beams bounced off the hallway wall.

'Taxi's here.'

'He's early.'

Adam drained the dregs of his wine glass and put it on the worktop before pulling her into an embrace.

'I'm going to miss you.'

'I'll miss you, too.'

The taxi driver honked the car horn.

'Someone's in a rush.'

'Yeah, I'd imagine the interchange with the M25's a nightmare this time of evening. Best not keep him waiting.'

He pulled away, and Kay followed him out to the hallway before opening the door for him as he wheeled his case over the step.

The driver popped the boot, and for a fleeting moment Kay thought of the woman who'd been brutally murdered.

She tried to clear the thought as Adam lifted his case into the back and slammed the lid shut.

He bent down, spoke to the driver, then returned from the car, his eyes serious.

'For goodness' sake, be careful, okay?'

'Don't worry,' she smiled, and kissed him. 'I'll still be here when you get back.'

'Make sure you are.'

He gave her arm a squeeze, then jogged round to the passenger door of the taxi and climbed in.

Kay waved as the car reversed out the driveway and into the lane, then shut the door as it powered away.

She slipped the two large bolts across the top and bottom of the panelling, then walked through to the kitchen and did the same for the back door.

She realised with a jolt that this was the first time she'd been alone in the house for any length of time since the Professional Standards investigation the previous year.

And the first time since she'd discovered someone had been spying on her.

Suddenly, the house seemed incredibly empty without Adam's presence.

As she pulled the blinds down over the window, she peered out into the darkness.

Was Demiri watching her now?

She gave the blinds a final tug, and realised her hands were shaking.

It was only three days.

'I'll be okay.'

# CHAPTER SIXTEEN

Kay pulled the seatbelt across her body and settled into the passenger seat of the car for the drive down to the coast the next morning.

While she checked her emails on her phone, Barnes manoeuvred the vehicle through the town centre, overtook a slow-moving truck and then turned down the radio once they were speeding through the Kentish countryside heading south.

'Any information on the garage owner?'

Kay dropped her phone into her bag and pulled out a bundle of papers that Debbie had handed to her on the way out the door. She flicked to the third page and skimmed her eyes over the contents.

'Reg Powers. Sixty-two years old. He's been the owner of the place since 1991. Before that, it belonged to his father-in-law, who passed away in 1993. Divorced, no kids. Tax records show he employs two part-time staff.'

'Business doing well?'

Kay shrugged. 'It's getting by. He's not going to break any records with his income, but that's not surprising given the location – he's not in a very built up area, and Debbie said there's a large new car dealership in Hythe that has a state of the art servicing business on the side, so a lot of people probably go there.'

'You think most of his customers are repeat ones, then?'

'Yeah, I reckon. Probably people that knew his father-in-law or have had their car serviced by him for years.'

'Does he sell many second-hand cars?'

Kay flipped the page. 'No – about eight a year.' She dropped the bundle into her lap and stared out the windscreen. 'Probably does it on the side as a bit of extra income if one of his customers wants to sell a car, or something like that.'

'We'll soon find out.'

Barnes changed down a gear and slowed as they approached the first in a line of villages they had to pass through to reach their destination.

'I haven't been down this way in years,' said Kay as she took in the small post office to her left and a corner shop that appeared to be struggling for business.

'We used to bring Emma down this way when she was little,' said Barnes. 'Not a great beach there, but she used to like paddling in the water when she was a toddler. Plus, there was always a decent pub on the way back to stop for a late lunch and she could play in the garden.'

They fell into a companionable silence for a few more miles, until Barnes cleared his throat.

'Have you seen Larch lately?'

Kay frowned. 'Actually, no. Maybe three weeks ago?'

'Doesn't that seem unusual to you? He's normally sniffing around the incident room on a daily basis waiting to have a go at someone.'

'I suppose there might be meetings and things happening we don't know about?'

Barnes grunted. 'I heard the Joint Intelligence Unit had an undercover operation going on. Maybe that's got something to do with it. You think he'd be involved in that?'

'Honestly, Ian – I don't care as long as he's leaving me alone. I've quite enjoyed the last few weeks without him breathing down my neck, quite frankly.'

Barnes grinned, and then jerked his chin over the steering wheel as he swung the car to the right. 'This is the place.'

Kay eased herself out of the car when Barnes parked, stretching her back while she waited for him to lock the doors.

The small garage had been built on a corner block on a road that led off from the main street of the village. Four cars were parked on the oil-specked concrete apron, all in various states of antiquity and disrepair.

Kay's eyes caught a glimpse of a tell-tale rainbow of

oil sparkling in a puddle, before she turned to Barnes as he snorted loudly.

He wrinkled his nose at the vehicles. 'Christ, that one on the left looks exactly like the heap of rust Emma tried to get me to buy her last week.'

'Driving lessons going well?'

'Yeah – takes her test next week. I'm not buying her a pile of crap though, that's for sure.'

'These look like they're being butchered for parts.'

'I bloody hope so. Look at the rust in the wheel arches of that one, for goodness' sake.'

Two faded blue corrugated iron doors had been pegged open, the garage space beyond lost to a dust mote-heavy gloom.

Kay and Barnes moved closer to the threshold, a pungent mix of aromas assaulting their senses – oil, grease, cigarette smoke – all vying for attention amongst a pervading stench of body odour.

Kay opened her mouth to call out, and then jumped at a phlegmy cough from behind them.

She spun round.

'Help you?'

The man before her pushed a dirty black baseball cap up his forehead and narrowed his eyes, his top lip curling.

'Police. I should've guessed, the way you're dressed. You stand out a mile.'

Kay flicked open her warrant card. 'Detective Sergeant Hunter. This is Detective Constable Barnes. And you are?'

'Reginald Powers. I'm the owner.' He pointed at a rusting logo nailed to the wall of the building alongside a rusting MOT accreditation sign.

He stalked past her, brushing her sleeve as he went, and pointedly ignored Barnes.

'We'd like to ask you some questions.'

'I'm sure you would,' he muttered over his shoulder.

'Enough.' Barnes stormed into the garage after him. 'Mr Powers, we'd appreciate some cooperation. I'm sure you'll understand we're busy people, like you, so unless you want me to call the DVLA and the tax office to request an immediate audit of your business, perhaps you'd afford my colleague here the attention and respect she deserves?'

The man held up his hands. 'There's no need for that.' His eyes shifted to Kay. 'I'm very busy, that's all.'

She cast her gaze around the garage, its double bay taken up by a solitary vehicle and the work benches along one wall covered with a variety of tools, all discarded haphazardly.

'Busy. Right.' She turned back to Powers and held out a copy of a vehicle registration certificate. 'Tell me about this car. Who did you sell it to?'

Powers snatched the document from her, extracted a pair of reading glasses from the pocket of his overalls and perched them on the bridge of his nose.

'Can't remember,' he said.

'Try harder,' said Barnes, and folded his arms across his chest.

Powers swallowed, glanced down at the page in his hand, and then back to Kay.

'Oh, that's right. A bloke from Maidstone way. A few months ago.' He held out the registration document. 'Is there a problem?'

'Where's your copy of the receipt?'

He shrugged. 'The office was broken into six weeks ago. A lot of paperwork was taken.'

'Did you report it?'

Another shrug. 'No. They didn't take anything of value. Any cash is kept in the safe. Probably just kids. Some of the tools were taken, too. Only the cheap ones, mind.'

'Did the car belong to you?'

'Yes.'

'Who did you buy it from?'

'Auctions at Sittingbourne.'

'Got the paperwork?'

'No – it got taken—'

'When you were burgled six weeks ago. Right.'

Powers shifted from foot to foot before wiping the back of his hand under his nose. He jerked his thumb over his shoulder.

'If that's all, I've got to get this vehicle's MOT sorted out today.'

Kay forced down her frustration, fished out one of her business cards from her bag, and handed it to the garage owner.

'If your memory returns, give me a call,' she said, and turned on her heel.

'And here's my card,' said Barnes. 'I'll expect a phone call from my colleagues at Hythe by the end of the week to tell me you've presented them with a full set of your licencing authority documents.'

Kay smiled as she made her way back to the car, Barnes's footsteps close behind.

Unlocking the car, he stabbed the key in the ignition and glared at the front of the garage.

'Lying bastard,' he spat.

'He is,' said Kay. 'Now all we have to do is find out why.'

# CHAPTER SEVENTEEN

Jozef Demiri folded his enormous frame into a large leather armchair and swirled the brandy around in his glass as his eyes flickered across the screen in front of him.

The exclusive club had had an invitation-only policy, and right now he was watching a replay of three of his more lucrative clients enjoying a private viewing. The woman who paraded in front of them was young, hand-picked, and had been one of his favourites.

He sighed, leaned forward and switched off the monitor as the phone at his elbow began to vibrate.

'What is it?'

He listened to the caller, and took a sip of the light brown liquid, savouring the flavours that caressed his tongue before he swallowed.

'Show him in.'

He ended the call, placed the crystal glass next to the phone and eased himself out of the chair.

Ignoring the boxes that had been placed against one wall, he made his way across to a desk at the centre of the room as the door to his private office opened, and Tavender appeared, his face thunderous.

'Well?' said Demiri.

'Millard and Hudson's prints were found on the car. They've been arrested.'

'Will they talk?'

A glint appeared in Tavender's eyes. 'Millard has a six-year-old girl at school in Gravesend. Hudson's girlfriend is pregnant. No, they won't talk, I can assure you.'

'They'd better not.' Demiri narrowed his eyes, his instincts alert. 'Was that all?'

Tavender's gaze shifted to the carpet, then back.

'Well?'

'Powers called. Hunter turned up at his place with another detective, Ian Barnes.'

'When?'

'This morning.'

'How the hell did they work that out?'

'They must've traced the vehicle back to him.'

Demiri fought to keep his voice calm. 'He has clear instructions what to do with the vehicles he provides, does he not?'

'Yes, Mr Demiri.'

'He's getting lazy. Is this the first time?'

Tavender looked away.

Demiri cleared the space between them in three paces, and slapped the man's face. 'Answer me! Don't you dare look away from me when I'm speaking to you.'

The man rubbed his cheek, but met Demiri's eyes. 'I'm sorry, Mr Demiri.'

Millard and Hudson were expendable. He had no doubt they'd maintain their silence for fear of what Tavender would do to their families, but Powers was an unfortunate case.

The man had no family, no commitments, and would therefore be unresponsive to any threats Tavender could make.

As it was, they had already arranged for the burglary six weeks ago to take care of some extracurricular business Powers had taken upon himself to run from the small garage.

Demiri had left the man in no doubt about his responsibilities to the organisation, and Powers had quickly acquiesced after Tavender had threatened to take a blowtorch to his balls.

If it had been anyone else, there would have been nothing left to salvage, but the garage owner had his uses – disposable vehicles were a rarity with all the rigorous controls exerted by the UK authorities, and finding another dealer would have been problematic at short notice.

Demiri drained his glass.

Unfortunately, it seemed Powers hadn't learned his lesson.

It was time he was taught a permanent one.

'End his engagement with us. Use him as an

example to show our other suppliers that when I give them instructions, they do as they're told.'

'Yes, Mr Demiri.'

'What about Stokes?'

'No more news. I'm monitoring the situation. If there's an opportunity to deal with him, we will.'

Demiri tapped his finger against the empty crystal glass, the soft chime from the gold ring on his right hand filling the air. 'We don't need these sorts of distractions. You should have dealt with him at the same time as the girl.'

The other man lowered his gaze. 'I'm sorry, Mr Demiri.'

'Don't get sloppy in your work, Tavender. I'm relying on you.'

The other man nodded, and straightened. 'I have some news regarding Detective Hunter.'

'Oh?'

'It appears the vet has left home for a while – he was seen getting into a taxi with a large suitcase.'

'Interesting.' Demiri rubbed his chin, then waved the other man away. 'Go now.'

Demiri waited until Tavender had closed the door behind him, then sank back into his armchair and ran his hand over his eyes.

A new shipment was due to arrive in days, the customers expectant, and the necessary arrangements in place to ensure a smooth transition. And yet, the organisation seemed frayed at the edges.

He ground his teeth.

Stokes's complacency could ruin it all, and Demiri only had himself to blame.

Tavender had come to him two months ago to say he'd been concerned about the driver; that he'd been spending too much time with one of the girls instead of minding his own business.

Demiri had dismissed it as a passing fancy – Stokes had been his driver for over a year, and he'd had no other reason to doubt the man.

Until now.

As for the shipment, they would have to use the vehicles they'd already kept under close watch, ready to meet his suppliers and transport the packages across the county.

His mind turned to the detective and her superior.

He had no doubt he'd be seeing more of her, and he ran his tongue over his lips with anticipation. The fact that she was at home alone excited him.

He closed his eyes, and exhaled.

Seven more days, and he could relax.

# CHAPTER EIGHTEEN

Kay flicked through the document in her hands, then tossed it onto her desk in disgust and sighed.

A sense of frustration had crawled through her veins as she'd sifted through the updated reports about Jozef Demiri's business interests. She knew most of them by rote; she'd memorised the facts and figures during the last investigation into the man, and only had to cast her eye over the additional facts for the past twelve months.

Yet, nothing had changed.

The man still maintained an impeccable façade while being responsible for most of the drug problems in the south-east corner of England.

Carys looked up from her computer. 'Nothing?'

'No.' Kay ran her hand through her hair and collapsed into her chair. 'Not on the official accounts, anyway. What about you?'

The younger detective shrugged, her eyes flickering over the screen in front of her. She wrinkled her nose.

'Nothing that's going to get us a search warrant for his offices, that's for sure. Couple of council notices relating to some signage being put up on the outside of the building that had to be taken down – it was against town planning laws, apparently. That's it.'

'Shame,' said Gavin from his position next to Barnes's desk.

Kay murmured her agreement, then glanced up as Sharp entered the incident room.

'Okay, you lot. Gather round. Let's get this briefing underway.'

Kay stretched her back as she made her way over to where the whiteboard had been set up, then perched on the corner of Debbie's desk.

The police officer smiled and passed a packet of biscuits to Kay, who grinned and took one.

'Thanks, Debs.'

Sharp turned his attention to Kay and Barnes once everyone had settled. 'How did you get on with the garage owner?'

'He was hard work,' said Kay. 'We suspect he's hiding something but I didn't want to press it too hard today and frighten him off. He says he can't remember who he sold the car to, and that he purchased it at the Sittingbourne auctions. However, he had a break-in a few months ago and all the documentation was stolen.'

'Too convenient,' added Barnes.

'Covering for someone?' said Carys.

'He didn't sound scared,' said Barnes. 'He was cocky; arrogant.'

'Protected by someone, maybe?' said Kay. 'Maybe by someone who'd be prepared to stage a break-in to remove documentary evidence of a vehicle sale?'

'Do you think he's dealing in stolen vehicles?' said Gavin.

'There's nothing in the system, but that's probably because he hasn't been caught – yet.'

'All right, keep digging,' said Sharp. 'There's got to be something there.' He peered down at his notebook on the desk beside him, and then turned back to the team.

'We have had one major development,' he said. 'Lucas sent over the results of the post mortem on our female victim an hour ago. Given the content of that report, I've spoken to him on the phone, but he maintains his position. She was alive when she was placed in the back of the car.'

A shockwave emanated from the team sat before him, and Kay's jaw dropped.

'Alive?'

Sharp nodded. 'That's what Lucas says. She was killed when the side of her head struck the metalwork of the car when it overturned – he says instantly. The base of her skull was caved in with the force of the impact.'

'So, she was conscious all the time she was in the boot of the car, wrapped in plastic?' said Gavin. 'I'm surprised she didn't suffocate.'

'I checked that with Harriet,' said Sharp. 'When we arrived on scene, the plastic had already been torn open by the impact – that's how we spotted her limbs, but Harriet says some small perforations had been made in the wrapping, near the woman's mouth. The post mortem results support this – whoever she is, she didn't die from asphyxiation because she managed to get enough air into her lungs to stay alive.'

'You'd have thought he'd have checked for that,' said Carys.

'True. Why wouldn't he?' said Kay.

'Could've had another kill site in mind to finish her off,' said Barnes, his face grim. 'It was only our assumption that he'd already killed her and was preparing to dump the body.'

'Hell of a risk,' said Gavin. 'If he'd been pulled over for erratic driving instead of crashing—'

Sharp rose from the desk and pinned two more photographs to the board, then took a step back so the team could see. He pointed to the first one, to the body of a skinny brunette woman, eyes closed, her skin bloated in death.

'This woman was found on the banks of the artificial lakes at Aylesford a year ago,' he said.

'I remember that,' said Barnes. 'No identification, and no-one had reported her missing.'

Sharp nodded. 'Signs of drug usage, too. No-one's ever been charged with her murder.' He tapped the second photograph, showing another young woman, this time with short blonde hair, a bruise covering her left cheek.

'This woman was found at the opposite end of the lake five months later. She didn't appear on any of the databases but the post mortem results showed she was severely malnourished, and probably living rough for a number of months leading up to her death. Both women were found wrapped in plastic. Those details were never released to the public, and the investigating officers have had no new leads to follow.'

Kay swallowed, the remnants of dry biscuit sticking in her throat. 'Were they alive when they were submerged?'

'The post mortem results confirm that they were, yes.'

'He's been lucky, if it's the same man responsible for all three deaths,' said Kay. 'That's a busy area to be dumping bodies.'

Sharp rubbed his chin. 'Or, he heard that these two bodies were found, and relocated,' he said. 'But to where?'

'You think there are more?' said Carys.

Sharp folded his arms across his chest and nodded. 'I do, yes. Everything points to someone who's had plenty of practice at this.'

'Bastard,' said Barnes. 'He'd bloody better survive surgery.'

# CHAPTER NINETEEN

Sharp lifted his gaze at a knock on the door to the incident room, and Kay glanced over her shoulder.

A nervous-looking young police constable stood on the threshold, his eyes scanning the room until he located Sharp.

'What is it, Constable?'

'The Chief Superintendent, sir. Wants a word with you and Detective Sergeant Hunter at headquarters. Said "immediately".'

All eyes turned to Kay, the hubbub of the briefing dying on the air as a shocked silence swept through the room.

Sharp's eyes narrowed as he glanced towards his office. 'I didn't hear my phone ring.'

'Message came through the switchboard,' said the constable. 'I explained you were probably in the middle of a briefing.'

'All right. We'll be right there.'

The constable nodded, and left the room in a hurry.

'Kay? My office. The rest of you, we've still got a murder investigation to manage, so don't let this interruption keep you from your work.' When no-one moved, he glared at them. 'That means now.'

Admin staff and detectives scurried to their desks as Kay grabbed her suit jacket from the back of her chair and followed Sharp into his office, closing the door behind her.

'Any idea what this is about?'

'No – do you?'

She shook her head.

'Well, unless Mr Demiri has filed a complaint – which I very much doubt – I'm as much in the dark as you, so let's go and see what the Chief Super has to say.'

He swung his jacket over his shoulders and they made their way back out through the incident room and down a flight of stairs.

Signing out for a pool car, Sharp drove the short distance to Kent Police Headquarters in record time, and led the way to the Chief Superintendent's office.

Kay rubbed her eye while Sharp stood at the office door, his hand poised and ready to knock.

He glanced over his shoulder at her.

'Ready?'

'Not really.' Kay swallowed. She'd never been summoned to the Chief Superintendent's office before.

Memories of standing outside a headmaster's office

after the rare occasion of a detention set by an impatient teacher sprang to mind.

She took a deep breath, let it out, and then nodded at Sharp.

There was a brief pause after he knocked, and then the Chief Superintendent's voice rang out.

'Come in.'

Kay brushed an errant loose hair off the shoulder of her jacket and followed Sharp into the room.

Susan Greensmith, Chief Superintendent for West Kent Division, rose from her seat as they entered, smiled and shook hands with Sharp, and then held out her hand to Kay.

'Thanks for coming, DS Hunter. Please, take a seat.'

She gestured to the chairs in front of the wide desk, and resumed her position behind it, pushing a pile of cardboard folders out of the way and clasping her hands in front of her.

'I understand you have a development in the case of the woman killed in the road traffic accident three nights ago, and that you suspect Jozef Demiri to be involved. What's the current status of your enquiries, Devon?'

Kay listened as Sharp provided a précis of their investigation while the chief superintendent interjected with questions and clarifications from time to time, and wondered why a face-to-face meeting had been requested when Sharp was already submitting daily reports.

Sharp finished speaking, and leaned back in his chair.

Greensmith pursed her lips. 'It certainly sounds like you and your team are doing everything possible with what information you have to hand, Devon.'

'Thank you.'

'However, I'm guessing that the pair of you are wondering why I've dragged you over here.'

Kay bit her lip as Sharp made a noncommittal noise at the back of his throat.

Greensmith unfolded her hands and gestured to the topmost file in her tray.

'I don't need to tell you both that the arrest and subsequent prosecution of Jozef Demiri have been high on our agenda, especially after what happened to you, Hunter.'

Heat rushed to Kay's cheeks, but she held her tongue.

Greensmith's tone was matter-of-fact rather than accusatory, and she continued as if oblivious to Kay's discomfort.

'The thing is,' the chief superintendent continued, 'our Serious and Organised Crimes Unit has never given up on Demiri, and in an attempt to draw on every resource I have available to me, recent events in your investigation lead me to one conclusion. SOCU should be leading all investigations into Jozef Demiri's business.'

'But—'

'I'm sorry, Detective Hunter, but SOCU are better equipped to deal with whatever Demiri can throw at us.'

'What does DCI Larch think of this?' said Kay, then bit her lip, realising she was pushing her luck.

Greensmith raised an eyebrow before responding. 'Not that it's any of your business, detective, but DCI Larch is currently leading another aspect of the investigation.'

'But—'

'That's all I'm prepared to tell you, Hunter.'

'Ma'am, if I could make a suggestion?' said Sharp.

'Go ahead.'

'Both Hunter and I are well versed in how dangerous Demiri can be. Rather than cut our team loose completely, perhaps we could be seconded to the SOCU investigation?'

'I did say you wouldn't hand this over without a fight, Devon.' She held up her hand to stop him interrupting. 'I understand the time and effort you put into pursuing this man over the years.'

She leaned forward and press the button on her phone. 'Louise? Send in DCI Harrison, please.'

Kay heard Sharp swear under his breath, and raised her eyebrow.

He shook his head, and they both stood as the door opened and a man entered the room, his height leaving scant room as he ducked instinctively under the door frame.

'DS Hunter, this is Detective Chief Inspector Simon Harrison. Sharp, I believe you and Harrison know each other?'

'We've met before.'

Greensmith waited until the introductions were complete, and then locked her computer screen and picked up her mobile phone from her desk.

'I'll leave it to the three of you to work out the arrangements. Keep it civil. I want my office back in one piece when I return in thirty minutes.'

Kay moved back to her chair but didn't sit down as the door closed behind Greensmith. Instead, she watched with interest as Sharp stood to one side to let Harrison cross to the window.

The tension between the two men was palpable, and she wondered what the history was between them. It was evident the outcome had left each with unresolved issues.

Harrison turned to face them, his hands clasped behind his back and a tight smile on his face.

'Well, Sharp, I didn't think our paths would cross again. Not like this.'

'You're looking well, Simon. How's Gravesend suiting you?'

Harrison grimaced, but recovered quickly. 'It gives me scope to monitor the bigger issues in Kent. I much prefer being involved on the frontline though.'

'We understand your SOCU team might want some assistance in putting together a case against Jozef Demiri,' said Kay.

Harrison turned his attention to her, his eyes sparkling.

'I've already seconded a detective sergeant from Maidstone police station to work on this case with me.'

'Oh. Who?'

'Jake O'Reilly.'

Kay managed to bite back the surprised outburst that threatened to escape her lips.

O'Reilly had a tenuous record at best when it came to his workload, and she reminded herself the DS still hadn't found out who had attacked Gavin Piper in the spring, leaving the younger detective in hospital with broken ribs.

She hadn't broached the subject before, reluctant because she blamed herself for the attack on Gavin. She had long suspected it had been a warning to her to drop her own enquiries into Demiri's business, and she had no wish to endanger her colleagues further.

She dug her nails into her palms.

'Kay's got a point,' said Sharp. 'My team has a better knowledge of the immediate vicinity and Demiri's known locations. We've already interviewed him in relation to the body of the woman found in a vehicle involved in an accident three nights ago, and we're waiting to interview the driver. We've got the manpower you're going to need and we're already mobilised.'

'I can work alongside O'Reilly to bring him up to speed with our investigation to date,' Kay added.

Harrison smirked. 'I don't think that's necessary, Hunter.'

'Why not? I've worked with the Major Crimes Unit for five years. I've been seconded to SOCU before, and I've undergone adequate training. I'm more than capable. Besides, you could say I've got a vested interest in how this all turns out, haven't I, guv?'

'I'm not sure what the Chief Super will have to say about this.'

Kay smiled, and folded her arms. 'Well, we could wait until she comes back and ask her?'

'Or you could phone her,' said Sharp. 'She seemed to know where to find you at a moment's notice, so I'm presuming you have her mobile number?'

Harrison's eyes narrowed, and he stalked towards the door. 'Wait here.'

Sharp leaned forward and lowered his voice as the door closed quietly behind the DCI. 'You don't have to do this, Kay. You know how dangerous Demiri is.' He held up a hand to silence her. 'I'm not denying your capabilities. I *am* questioning the sense in having you so close to someone who's already proved he's not above breaking into your house and possibly attacking your colleague in an attempt to stop you pursuing him.'

'I want this,' said Kay. 'For my daughter, and everything else. I want justice.'

She turned her attention at a polite cough from Harrison, who stood in the doorway.

He raised an eyebrow at her and Sharp, then his lips thinned into a brief semblance of a smile.

'I can't say I'm entirely surprised by your demands, Hunter. I always did get the impression you were obsessive in your pursuit of Demiri.'

Kay swallowed, but remained silent as he turned his attention to Sharp.

'Your team can remain on the investigation into the woman's death,' he said. 'And, you'll be seconded to me until we see Demiri charged.'

'Thank you,' Kay breathed.

Harrison's top lip curled. 'There won't be another chance if you change your mind, Hunter. We're going after him. Now.'

# CHAPTER TWENTY

'Are you going to tell us who the man in the hospital is?'

Simon Harrison folded his arms across his chest. 'Daniel Stokes is the name Demiri knows him by.'

'What do you mean?'

The man sighed, and contemplated his fingernails. 'I suppose it doesn't matter now if you know his name. He won't be working undercover anymore, and we're probably going to have to construct a new identity for him after this latest debacle. His real name is Gareth Jenkins. He's a detective sergeant who's been working undercover in Demiri's organisation for the past two years. A highly valuable asset, too it must be said.'

'Who's the dead girl? Do you know?' asked Sharp.

'Gareth would have to confirm, but I strongly suspect from looking at the photographs it's an illegal entrant from Romania called Katya.'

'It's not an "it", it's "she",' said Kay. 'How do you

know her name?'

'We've been monitoring Demiri, as I said, for two years now. When we started the operation, we believed him to be responsible for a large amount of drugs being smuggled into the country via the south Kent coastline. Gareth's remit was to get himself positioned within Demiri's business and gain access to information about how the drugs were being imported, and by whom.'

Kay frowned. 'The truck we found the gun in?'

Harrison nodded. 'That was one way – the trucks were brought in by ferry rather than through the Channel Tunnel. The ferry traffic is harder to control – understaffing and the like means we can only carry out spot checks most of the time, unless we've received a tip-off. The Tunnel's sexier to terrorists, so that's where most of our resources are placed. The truck you're referring to was impounded after your investigation was concluded—'

Kay glared at him. 'It wasn't concluded. I was set up.'

He held up a hand. 'I'm sorry. If I could continue? Once we had the truck, we sent our own crime scene investigators back over it. Yours had done a fantastic job, but their focus was on linking Demiri to the gun and any drug residue. We were looking for something else.'

'What?'

'Evidence to show that Jozef Demiri is running a successful business in people trafficking. More specifically, slavery and prostitution.'

'Did they find anything?' asked Sharp.

'Oh, yes. Hair, traces of blood, faeces, you name it – only in minute quantities though.' He shook his head. 'It took an age. I'll be honest, we thought he was going to get away with it at one point. Gareth had warned us Demiri always insisted on each vehicle being thoroughly cleaned after each shipment.'

Kay exhaled and pushed herself out of her chair to walk over to the window.

To hear Harrison talk about Demiri's victims so dispassionately sent a shiver down her neck, and she crossed her arms before turning her back onto the sunshine streaming through the blinds.

'What happened to Katya?'

A look of distress stole across Harrison's features, and he cleared his throat before speaking.

'We always warn them,' he said. 'Our officers, I mean. Not to get involved. They can't risk having ties with anyone, doing that sort of work. It's why we approached Gareth. He has no parents, no siblings, no wife or girlfriend to worry about or who Demiri could use if his cover was blown. We always tell them not to get married or have a serious relationship.' He sighed and ran a hand through his hair, suddenly looking weary. 'It never ends well. Unfortunately, Gareth seems to have fallen for Katya, and told us at our last debrief that he meant to get her away from Demiri. Told us she knew things that would help us put Demiri away for life.'

'What sort of things?' said Kay.

'We don't know. She refused to tell him until we

guaranteed her safety. She was terrified of Demiri, and wouldn't speak until we undertook to get her out of there.'

'What went wrong?' said Sharp.

Harrison shrugged. 'We think Demiri found out about them.'

'You think?' said Kay. She strode across the room, snatched up the cardboard folder Greensmith had placed in her correspondence tray, and pulled out the photograph of Katya's body in the back of the car before waving it under Harrison's nose. 'Seems to me he *did* find out.'

Colour rose on Harrison's face. 'She must've said something to someone.'

'Or they were both under surveillance,' said Sharp. 'Demiri knew what Gareth was up to and used her to send you a message.'

'When did you find out about Gareth's accident?' said Kay.

'He didn't contact me at his scheduled time four nights ago.'

'And yet, it's taken you until now to inform us,' said Sharp through gritted teeth, his eyes blazing.

Kay looked to Sharp, then back to Harrison. 'We need to talk with him as soon as he's awake.'

'I seem to be able to pre-empt your demands with uncanny accuracy,' said Harrison. 'Gareth woke up three hours ago. You're scheduled to meet with him the moment we're finished here.'

'Well, what the hell are we waiting for?'

# CHAPTER TWENTY-ONE

Kay wasn't surprised when Harrison insisted on driving, but she was taken aback when their vehicle shot past the junction for Barming and kept going.

Sharp had requisitioned the front passenger seat, so she had to lean forward from her position behind Harrison.

'Where are we going? I thought Jenkins was at Maidstone Hospital?'

His eyes flickered to the rear-view mirror, then back to the road. 'We had him moved under sedation last night. I insisted on an embargo on the news until we'd had a chance to speak.'

'Why?'

'Maidstone's too big. Too easy for Demiri to cause a distraction and get to Gareth. We've had him moved to a small private hospital outside Tunbridge Wells.'

'Are they equipped to look after him?' said Sharp.

'Yeah. State of the art emergency facilities and

intensive care unit. He's in the best hands the taxpayer could afford, in the circumstances.'

'Does he know about Katya?'

'He was informed when he regained consciousness, yes.'

Kay leaned back in her seat and stared out the window as the countryside flew past and sighed.

Sharp glanced over his shoulder. 'You okay?'

'Yeah.'

The rest of the journey was completed in silence, only broken by Harrison announcing their arrival near the private hospital as he indicated off a roundabout and joined a bypass on the outskirts of the spa town.

Five minutes later, they were striding across a car park past ornamental landscaping, and then down the side of the three-storey modern building.

Two security guards stood next to a rear fire exit, and straightened as Harrison approached.

He pulled out his warrant card and turned back to Kay and Sharp as one of the guards brought his radio to his lips.

'I meant what I said. We're not taking any chances. No-one knows he's here except us. These people don't know who they're guarding.'

'Where'd you find them?' said Kay.

'They're serving officers in our Tactical Response Unit,' said Harrison. 'There are four more of them inside the building, two of whom are inside Gareth's room.'

As the guard finished talking and cleared his throat, Kay met Sharp's eyes.

Suddenly, everything Harrison had told her about Demiri's business and his determination to remain above the law seemed very, very real.

'This way,' barked Harrison.

Sharp held the door open for her, then followed as they made their way along a narrow corridor and up a flight of stairs.

Despite the sweeping smoked glass along the front of the medical facility, the rear of the building was featureless and functional and Kay noted signs pointing to administration offices and storerooms as she kept up with Harrison.

They turned a corner, and Kay peered around Harrison to see two more armed guards halfway along the next corridor.

One of them pivoted to face them as they neared, and Kay shuffled from foot to foot as their identification was checked once more.

Finally, the guard waved them past and pointed to a door on the left.

'Thanks,' said Harrison.

He pushed open the door and beckoned to them to follow.

As Kay passed him and into the room, she took a sharp intake of breath.

A man lay on a single bed to the left-hand side of the door, a series of tubes and wires protruding from under the blankets as machines next to the bed beeped and whirred.

Two armed guards stood to the right of the room, and Harrison waved them outside.

'Stay by the door, though.'

The taller of the two nodded, and pulled the door shut behind them.

Sharp circled the end of the bed, his face impassive while Harrison approached the man in the bed.

'Gareth? It's Simon Harrison. We wanted a quick word.'

The man's eyes flickered open, and his eyes swept the three faces that stared at him until his gaze found Kay.

'So, you're Kay Hunter, huh?' He managed a small smile. 'I'd say it's nice to meet you properly at last, but—'

'Yeah, I know. Circumstances.' Kay shrugged. She had no time for niceties. She folded her arms across her chest. 'What did Katya tell you about Demiri's business that got her killed?'

Jenkins swallowed, lowered his eyes and shook his head.

Kay glanced up at Sharp, who nodded.

'The thing is, Gareth, our pathologist tells us she wasn't dead while she was in the boot of your car. She was just unconscious. The force of the car crash killed her. So, where were you going with her? Did you decide she'd outlived her usefulness?'

A single tear rolled down the man's cheek.

Kay swallowed. She hated the line of questioning, but she and Sharp needed answers, and so did Harrison.

'The bastard,' he rasped.

He wiped at his eyes and glared at her. 'He has another man that works closely with him – Oliver Tavender. He phoned me four days ago and told me to have the car ready at the back of his nightclub in Maidstone town centre. When I got there, he told me to stay in the car. I watched him in the mirrors. He dragged something towards the back of it, opened the boot, and then came back round to where I was sitting and told me to dump it in woodland the other side of Ryarsh.'

'What caused the crash?' said Sharp. 'Early indications from the crash investigators are that there was nothing on the road to cause you to swerve. Even the truck driver that was parked on the hard shoulder said the car went out of control for no apparent reason.'

Jenkins sniffed. 'I'd already decided earlier that night to get Katya away from Demirl. She knew stuff way too much about his business. I knew she was in danger.' He glanced at Harrison, his eyes contrite. 'I know I shouldn't have got involved, but I couldn't help it. I knew I had to dump whatever was in the boot of the car first though, otherwise Tavender would've got suspicious. I was driving down the motorway, and I used my own mobile to phone Katya. I wanted to warn her, to tell her that I'd be at her place within the hour and that I'd take her away.'

'Where to?' asked Harrison.

'I don't know!' Jenkins spat. 'I just knew I had to get her away.'

'What happened?' said Kay.

'I couldn't get a signal to start off with, and then when the call went through, I could hear a phone ringing in the back of the car.' He choked out a sob. 'I knew then that he'd killed her, and that it was her body that Tavender had put in the boot. They'd found out she'd talked to me. I was in shock. I-I just remember staring at the phone, trying to process what I was hearing, and then I looked up and saw the truck on the hard shoulder. I was too close. I—'

The machine next to the bed starting beeping at an alarming rate, and Kay reached out and touched Jenkins's shoulder. 'I'm so sorry, Gareth. We had to know.'

He nodded, and wiped at his eyes once more.

'What about the two women whose bodies were found near Aylesford last year?' said Sharp. 'Did you dump those?'

Jenkins shook his head. 'I've got no idea who was responsible for them,' he said. 'I'm not the only one Demiri uses.'

'What exactly did Katya tell you?' said Kay. She gestured to Harrison. 'Apparently, you never got to make your last report.'

Jenkins glanced across at Harrison, who nodded.

'It's okay, Gareth. They're on the investigating team now. We need to pool our resources to put Demiri away once and for all.'

'We understand he's involved in people smuggling,' said Sharp.

Jenkins let out a sigh that wracked his whole body. 'It's worse than that. I found out from Katya what goes on at that nightclub of Demiri's. I was meant to be meeting Harrison that night, and that's when I was going to tell him. Demiri's running a kill club.'

'A what?'

'He has a secret room there. Invitation only. There's maybe five or six clients that are the only ones who know about it. One of them flies in from Europe especially.'

Sharp moved closer to the bed. 'What sort of room?'

Jenkins's face turned paler. 'A torture chamber,' he whispered. 'Demiri's clients pay to pick a girl from each new boatload that's smuggled in. He's making a fortune from letting them live out their sick fantasies.'

Kay gasped, bile rising in her throat.

She dug her fingers into her palms, her nails biting into the soft skin as she closed her eyes and tried to keep calm, when all she wanted to do was run out to the car and drive back to Ashford and confront Demiri.

She swallowed, then opened her eyes.

Both Sharp and Harrison wore distraught expressions, and she knew they would feel as sick as she.

'We need to get a search warrant for that building immediately,' said Sharp to Harrison.

'I'll sort it out. Can you provide additional officers?'

'Absolutely. I'll get onto our crime scene investigators and arrange for them to meet us there.'

'It'll take a while to get the paperwork done.' Harrison checked his watch. 'It's too late to do anything tonight. Suggest a seven o'clock briefing tomorrow morning?'

Sharp nodded. 'We'll make some phone calls and make sure everyone's on time.' He turned to Jenkins. 'Thank you.'

As Kay turned away from the bed, Gareth's hand shot out and his fingers wrapped around her wrist.

'You listen to me,' he said, his voice fierce. 'You get him, and you make him pay for it. All of it, do you understand?'

Kay held his gaze.

'Yes,' she said. 'I understand.'

# CHAPTER TWENTY-TWO

Kay slid the empty plate across the desk, dusted crumbs from her lap and took a sip of wine before scooting her chair closer to her computer screen.

She'd worry about fixing a proper dinner later; cheese and biscuits were all she needed to sustain her while she worked through the notes she'd collated over the past eighteen months about Jozef Demiri.

When she'd first arrived home, she'd put on a sweatshirt and leggings and taken off at a brisk run past the pub and then across a mini roundabout that intersected the modern housing estate that had sprung up twenty years ago either side of the lane. Picking up her pace, she'd worked her legs hard, burning off the anger and frustration about Harrison taking over the case until she circled back and reached her front door forty minutes later, her breathing ragged and her thoughts clear.

She had to push back any grudges until they'd

caught Demiri. She had another chance to make the Albanian pay for what he'd done to her, let alone what he'd done to the poor women he'd smuggled in from the Continent, and she wouldn't rest until he was sentenced.

Now, she leaned forward and turned down the rock music that had been blasting out of the speakers so she could concentrate and rested her chin in one hand, the other using the mouse to click and scroll through the files.

The house seemed quiet without Adam.

When she'd got home from her run and before stepping into the shower, she'd locked all the doors, checked the garage door was secure and the door from the garage to the kitchen had been fastened shut, and then pressed all the buttons on the panel next to the front door to set the security lights.

Normally, when he was home, she'd be able to hear the television downstairs where he'd be watching a documentary or a football game. She'd be able to breathe in the aromas from his cooking, and wait for him to shout up the stairs that her dinner was getting cold.

She smiled. Adam was the better cook out of the pair of them and was happy to be left alone in the kitchen most nights – if she tried to help, he grumbled that she cut the vegetables the wrong way, or simply hid his eyes while she wielded the knife, unable to watch as she sliced with much gusto but very little finesse – or regard for her own safety.

A sound reached her ears and she straightened in her seat, her head cocked to one side.

There it was again.

A knock at the door.

She switched off the music, checked her watch and frowned.

Pushing her chair back from the desk, she made her way out to the landing. Ahead of her, the bright security lights shone through the curtains that covered the front windows.

She paused, raising her gaze to the ceiling.

A few months ago, she'd discovered a set of miniature cameras and microphones in the roof of her house that had been set up to spy on her through the spotlights in the ceiling. A quiet word with Sharp about her conviction that Demiri, or someone associated with him was responsible for their installation, led to the equipment being removed – carefully, and in such a way that the perpetrators would simply believe the cameras had failed due to a power outage.

Now she wondered whether her enemies had been watching her home more closely, and in person.

She swallowed, and then uttered a low cry at another loud knock on the door.

Staying close to the wall, she edged her way down the stairs, her heart racing.

She had nothing to use as a weapon, but her fingers found her mobile phone tucked into the back pocket of her jeans and she extracted it, her thumb hovering over the emergency button as she reached the foot of the stairs.

Kay cursed the frosted glass at the top of the door that prevented her from seeing who was standing on the doorstep. She thought she heard murmured voices, and then took hold of the handle and wrenched open the door at the same time as taking a step backwards.

'Food!'

Kay exhaled and dropped her hand from the door.

On the doorstep, Ian Barnes held four large pizza boxes in his arms. Behind him, Gavin and Carys stood, grinning from ear to ear.

Barnes lowered the boxes. 'You forgot it was your turn, didn't you?'

'My turn?'

'She forgot,' said Carys, and laughed. 'Told you she had.'

'Hurry up and let us in. It's cold out here.'

Kay stood back as her three colleagues tumbled over the threshold, laughing as they unwrapped scarves and threw their jackets over the newel post of the staircase before threading their way towards the kitchen.

She shook her head, smiled at her own paranoia, and closed the front door.

She pushed the bolts back into place and padded after them.

'Okay, I admit it – I forgot,' she said as she opened the refrigerator door and pulled out white wine and cans of beer.

Gavin collected glasses from the cupboard under the

worktop, and then lined them up and waited while Kay poured the drinks.

'Oh, guinea pigs!' Carys crouched next to the hutch. 'What're their names?'

Barnes and Gavin laughed when Kay told them.

'Can I pick them up?'

'You can pick up Bonnie,' said Kay. 'She's the little black and white one – Clyde's got a skin infection so I'm on nurse duties at the moment until Adam gets back from Aberdeen.'

Delighted, Carys flipped open the hatch and gently lifted Bonnie from where she'd been gazing up at the young detective.

'Aw, she's cute.'

Kay smiled as Carys cradled the animal against her stomach and scratched it between the ears. Her geriatric pet gerbil had died the previous month, and the woman had been inconsolable for days, especially when it transpired she had nowhere to bury her pet because she rented an apartment on the outskirts of town.

When he'd heard about her predicament, Adam had taken pity on her and offered to dig a grave for the gerbil at the bottom of their garden. Carys had been overwhelmed by the gesture, and had bought a new rose bush for them to mark the spot.

'She's not cute at half past four in the morning when she's hungry,' said Kay, and handed Carys a pre-made bag of raw vegetables from the refrigerator. 'Here, pop her back and give them this. Your pizza's getting cold.'

Carys washed her hands, then slid the roll of paper

kitchen towel into the centre of the worktop and sat on one of the bar stools with a loud sigh. 'That was a long day.'

Kay passed around the drinks. 'Cheers, you lot.'

They clinked glasses, and then Barnes flipped open the pizza boxes.

'Let's eat.'

They fell silent for a few minutes as they devoured the food, save for Barnes and Carys bickering about whether pineapple belonged on top of a pizza or not.

Kay took a sip of her wine, savouring the food and the easy company.

'That's better,' said Gavin, wiping his fingers on a piece of the kitchen towel before tossing it into one of the empty boxes.

'Didn't you eat today?' said Carys.

'Didn't have time.'

'Sharp'll moan at you,' said Kay. 'Have another slice – I'm stuffed.'

'He can't talk – I reckon he's the worst out of all of us.'

'What happened today?' said Barnes. 'Get your arse kicked again?'

Kay slapped his arm. 'No.'

She fell silent, lost in thought until Barnes nudged her.

'Come on. It's us.'

She managed a small smile, then took a sip of wine and set the glass down.

'A DCI Harrison from SOCU is taking over the Demiri case.'

A silence descended on the kitchen, only broken by a piece of mushroom falling off the pizza slice Gavin held halfway to his mouth.

He scooped it off the worktop and popped it into his mouth. 'Well, that's just bloody typical, isn't it?'

'Why would he do that to us?' demanded Barnes.

'To protect someone. The driver of that car crash.'

Everyone started talking at once, and after a few seconds Kay held up her hand.

'Look, Sharp will explain everything at tomorrow morning's briefing, but the driver's name is Gareth Jenkins. He was working for Jozef Demiri under an alias as part of an operation SOCU have been running for the past two years. He suspects Demiri found out that he was trying to save a girl – an illegal entrant – from some sort of private club Demiri runs.' She took a deep breath, and a shiver wracked her body. 'Jenkins alleges Demiri and the clients of that club are murdering young women. We persuaded Harrison to second us to his investigation, given that the girl died on our patch. Sharp and Harrison are getting a warrant organised tonight, so I'd imagine we'll be involved in the search sometime tomorrow.'

A silence filled the kitchen when she finished talking, and three shocked faces stared back at her.

'Christ, Kay,' said Barnes eventually. 'You don't do things by halves, do you?'

# CHAPTER TWENTY-THREE

Kay glanced up from her desk as Gavin pushed open the incident room door, his hair still wet from the shower.

'In early, Sarge?' he said as he passed, leaving a waft of shampoo in his wake.

'Yeah. Couldn't sleep.'

A faint smile crossed his lips. 'Me neither. Decided an early morning run might do me good.' He dumped his backpack under his desk and switched his computer on. 'I'm going to make a cup of tea – do you want one?'

'Cheers, thanks.'

Kay checked the clock on the right-hand side of her computer screen. She had ten minutes before Sharp began the planned meeting.

She'd realised overnight as she lay tossing and turning that whatever they discovered at the nightclub, it would mean days if not weeks of paperwork and on the ground investigation, and so she'd arrived early to make sure she delegated as much of her current workload as possible.

A DS over at headquarters was going to get a nasty surprise when he turned up for work in another thirty minutes, and she signed off her email with a promise of a favour returned.

She pressed "send" and crossed her fingers that her memory of his somewhat casual timekeeping was correct.

With any luck, the briefing would be well on its way by the time he received her note, and then it would be too late – she'd be out conducting the search with the rest of her colleagues.

Movement out the corner of her eye caught her attention and she bit back a retort of surprise as DS Jake O'Reilly swaggered through the incident room towards her, a sly grin on his face.

'Hunter. Still stuck here in the back of beyond?'

She fixed a smile to her face. 'O'Reilly. Any of that SOCU training rubbed off on you yet?'

His features clouded, and he paused at her shoulder.

Older than her by at least ten years, his greying mousy-coloured hair had been clipped too short at the sides recently, giving his head a pointed look and accentuating his large ears. Pale eyes narrowed as his top lip curled.

'I knew you'd be like this, Hunter. Jealousy won't get you anywhere. You and Sharp? Your days are numbered. No wonder the Chief Super had to get *my*

DCI involved. No doubt we'll have this case wrapped up in no time.'

'Good,' said Kay, keeping her smile sweet. 'Perhaps then you could pick up where you left off here and get around to finding out who attacked Piper six months ago.'

Gavin looked up at his name, then back to his work.

Kay couldn't blame him for ignoring O'Reilly – his nose had been left at a permanent soft angle after he was attacked in a car park close to the police station.

O'Reilly had been placed in charge of the ensuing investigation, but had gained no traction on his enquiries before disappearing from sight – and now Kay was still smarting from the news at his secondment to SOCU.

She set her jaw. No doubt the snub had been another jibe by DCI Larch to remind her of the Professional Standards investigation against her some eighteen months before, despite her innocence being upheld.

The door to the incident room swung open and Carys entered, a tray of takeaway coffee between her hands.

She stopped, the door bumping into her elbow as she spotted O'Reilly.

'Well, if it isn't the delightful DC Miles,' he said, turning away from Kay as he looked Carys up and down.

'DS O'Reilly. I-I didn't expect to see you here.'

Kay watched with bemusement as Carys blushed, and fiddled with the strap of her handbag as it tried to slide down her arm.

'Here, let me help you,' said O'Reilly, and rushed to her side.

'Oh, I'm sorry. I didn't get you a coffee.'

'No problem,' he soothed.

'Black, one sugar, isn't it? Same as me?' Carys emitted a giggle. 'You can have mine if you like?'

He winked. 'All right, but only if you're sure. Next one's on me though.'

Kay looked away, her eyes meeting Gavin's as he shook his head in disbelief and mimed putting his fingers down his throat.

It raised a smile, and she fought down the frustration that threatened common sense.

Barnes breezed in moments later, nodded to O'Reilly, took the coffee Carys handed to him and sank into his seat opposite Kay's desk.

'You've got a face like thunder. Morning get off to a good start, did it?'

Kay's retort was cut short by their DI turning up to begin the briefing.

'Who's the other bloke with Sharp?' whispered Barnes.

'That's the guy I told you about – Simon Harrison.'

Barnes said nothing, raised an eyebrow and spun his chair round to face the front of the room.

After introducing Harrison to the team, Sharp spent the next twenty minutes updating them about their meeting with Gareth Jenkins and his allegation that Demiri was running a people smuggling ring – and worse.

He paused to allow everyone time to catch up with their notetaking before continuing.

'We've obtained search warrants for Demiri's nightclub and we'll be conducting that search after this briefing,' he said.

'What about his house and offices?' asked Kay.

'The magistrate was reluctant to let us have warrants on the basis of hearsay,' said Harrison, a note of disgust in his voice. 'Her opinion is that Jenkins may have a personal vendetta against Demiri because of the death of Katya. Unless and until we find evidence at the nightclub to substantiate his claim, we won't get a warrant for the other premises.'

Barnes snorted, and crossed his arms over his chest. 'So, in the meantime, Demiri gets to come and go as he pleases.'

Harrison's mobile phone started to ring, and he glanced at the number, then Sharp. 'I have to take this.'

He gestured to Sharp to continue the briefing, and moved to the DI's office to take the call.

'Right, let's sort the teams out for the search on the nightclub while we're waiting for Harrison,' said Sharp. 'You know the routine – stab vests, the lot. SOCU will be leading the raid, but they're understaffed, too, so we need to support them in every way we can. O'Reilly – Harrison's got you paired with Barnes so you can act as liaison for both of us. You'll be posted towards the back of the cordon to start off with until the raid is underway.'

He proceeded to split the team into groups of two, with Kay being paired with Carys.

The younger detective pushed her chair over to where Kay sat so they could take notes together and pinpoint any prior knowledge of the area over and above the intelligence Harrison's team had already gathered.

Kay always admired Sharp's attention to detail and his ability to focus his team. With his military background, he was able to give clear orders without wasting words, and an intense atmosphere descended on the incident room as they listened to him.

Kay shifted her gaze as Harrison returned from Sharp's office, his face pale.

Sharp paused mid-sentence. 'Everything okay?'

Harrison moved to the front of the room, put his mobile in his pocket, and leaned against the desk closest to the whiteboard.

'That was the hospital,' he said, his eyes downcast. 'Gareth Jenkins passed away twenty minutes ago. Despite their best efforts to resuscitate him, he succumbed to his internal injuries and there was nothing they could do to save him.'

A silence fell on the room as the news sank in.

Kay's thoughts returned to the conversation she'd had with Jenkins the previous day.

*You get him, and you make him pay for it.*

She clenched her fist, her nails digging into her palm.

'We're all sorry to hear that,' said Sharp after a few moments.

'He knew the risks.' Harrison cast his gaze around the room. 'Are we ready?'

'We're ready,' said Sharp.

Harrison straightened, and adjusted his jacket. 'All right. Let's go.'

As the team began to move back to their desks and prepared to head to the stores room to obtain stab vests and the other paraphernalia that would be required prior to leaving to conduct the search, Sharp gave a low whistle.

Kay and the others turned and faced the front of the room where he stood stock-still beside the whiteboard.

'An officer gave his life to try and put Demiri away,' he said. 'Let's make this count.'

# CHAPTER TWENTY-FOUR

Kay tugged at the collar of her stab vest and tried to ignore the surge of adrenalin that seized at her heart as she listened to Harrison's final instructions.

She cast her eyes over the graffiti tags that littered the walls of the buildings, bright colours defying the worn dark bricks interspersed with simpler, spray-painted profanities, and wondered if any of the artists ever found real work in their chosen medium. Although she hated to admit it, at least two of the culprits had exceptional talent.

To her left, Carys shifted from foot to foot, her impatience emanating across the space between them.

Kay made a mental note to keep the younger detective in check. They'd been in a situation before where her colleague's enthusiasm for justice had nearly cost her life.

She peered over Carys's head to where Barnes and

O'Reilly stood, their expressions impassive as they watched Harrison send Gavin and two other men running to the locked front and rear doors of the nightclub.

From their position at the end of the alleyway that ran behind the building, Kay could make out a series of dirty windows that would've provided a view of the raid, except for the fact that grime covered the panes beyond the steel bars that filled the frames.

A Chinese takeaway had once been housed in the section of the building closest to where she stood, but she knew the family that owned it had been hounded away by Demiri's thugs over a year ago. The property on the opposite side of the nightclub hadn't housed a tenant in nearly five years.

Her right eye twitched, and she resisted the urge to rub at it. She refocused on her breathing, waiting for the command to proceed.

Any minute—

A crash echoed off the walls of the alleyway as the back door to the nightclub was breached, closely followed by a similar sound from the front of the building.

Kay edged forward on her toes, and heard Carys's sharp intake of breath.

'Come on,' she muttered.

A crackle of static burst to life through the radio in Sharp's hand, and he muttered a response to the team in the building before turning his attention to the waiting police officers.

'We're clear to proceed.'

He led them past three overflowing industrial-sized waste bins, the stink of waste assaulting Kay's nostrils as she tried not to think about the poor crime scene investigator who would be tasked with sifting through the contents.

A distinct stench of urine clung to the pitted surface under her feet and she grimaced as a large rat scurried across her path before disappearing through a gap under a padlocked door.

In moments, they were at the breached back entryway to the nightclub.

'Right, you've had a chance to look at the plans for the place,' said Sharp. 'Kay and Carys, I want you to search the ground floor offices. Take Dave Morrison and Aaron Stewart with you to record what you find. Keep your eyes open for anything that might give us some indication as to when another lot of people are arriving.'

'Guv.' Kay signalled to two uniformed officers to join them and led the way along an unlit corridor towards what would have been the nightclub manager's office.

She'd only met Morrison and Stewart after the morning's briefing had concluded. After quick introductions though, she was convinced of their capabilities and training – DCI Harrison would have insisted on only his most trusted people to carry out the raid, and they seemed as focused and keen as she that Demiri be locked away.

'What do you think our chances are of finding something if he knows about Jenkins?' said Carys.

'Slightly less than zero, but it's got to be done,' said Kay. She squinted as the lights overhead flickered to life. 'Seems they forgot to turn the power off before closing up.'

'Thank Christ for that,' said Stewart. 'Didn't fancy doing this by torchlight.' He flipped his torch into his utility belt and pulled on gloves. 'Ready when you are, Sarge.'

Kay nodded, and pushed against the door to the office.

It swung open freely, and she reached inside and flipped the light switch.

A strip of fluorescent lights flashed twice across the ceiling before saturating the office with a pale white hue.

A window to Kay's right provided a view across the club's dance floor, and she realised as she watched her colleagues moving across it towards the bar and the rooms beyond that it was mirrored on the other side. The manager could keep an eye on proceedings unnoticed.

A liquor cabinet had been placed under the window, while a two-seater leather sofa to one side of it still held the indentation of where someone had recently sat.

To her right, three filing cabinets stood against the wall, the drawers open and paper strewn across the floor. The desk in front of her was in a similar state and above that, a wall safe yawned open, its contents missing.

Kay sighed, and raised the radio to her lips. 'Guv? Looks like the place has been deserted in a hurry.'

Static spat through the speaker before Sharp responded. 'The bar and front area of the club has been stripped, too. We've missed them. You know what to do.'

'Got it.' She turned to the officers beside her and clipped the radio to her belt. 'Okay, split up. Dave, Aaron – you take the filing cabinets. Carys, help me see if we can salvage anything from the desk and drawers.'

They worked in silence, the sounds of their colleagues working their way through the rest of the club reaching Kay's ears as she sifted through the day-to-day workings of a busy town venue.

Suppliers' receipts, copies of licences for serving alcohol and late night openings were all she found to the side of the desk. She lifted her gaze to where Carys was making an inventory of the remainder, and pushed the tidied stacks of invoices towards her.

'We're going to be here for days,' Carys grumbled.

Kay didn't respond. Instead, she stretched her back and peered around at the room once more.

The decor appeared to have been well kept; the paintwork to the panelled walls appeared fresh, and even Kay had to admit the artwork on the walls was tasteful.

Compared with the dingy back of the club they'd entered through, this room was designed to impress.

Her thoughts returned to her conversation with Gareth Jenkins the day before.

If Demiri was providing an exclusive service to some of his clients, and the sort of service was what Jenkins had alleged, then they'd expect a certain level of luxury to their surroundings, she'd bet.

She turned and stared through the window to the public area of the club, then back to the room, and frowned.

She tugged her radio from her belt.

'Guv? Has anyone found anything to substantiate Gareth's claims?'

'Negative. Not yet.'

'Okay, thanks.'

She shoved the radio back into place and exhaled.

'Sarge? Might have something here.'

She spun on her heel to see Stewart jerking his thumb over his shoulder at the panelled walls next to the safe.

Kay frowned, and moved closer. 'What's that?'

He stood to one side so she could see, and pointed at a metal clasp set between two panels.

'I've seen something like this before. At a bloke's place in Lenham. He was a banker in the city, and he got burgled one night – bundled his wife and two kids into a custom-built panic room. The hinges on it looked like this.'

Kay ran a gloved hand over the silver-coloured clasp.

'Any idea how to get it open?'

'If it's been sealed from the inside, then we haven't got a chance in hell of doing it ourselves,' he said. 'But otherwise, if we apply pressure to the panels like this, we might find a way.'

He pushed his palm against the indented panel next to the clasp, but nothing happened.

'All right. Let's do this systematically,' said Kay. 'You start from that corner. I'll take this one. We move in a grid pattern, got it?'

She was aware of Carys and Morrison moving beside them, but kept her focus on the panels as she and Stewart worked their way across the wall.

Finally, after she was almost ready to concede defeat, a faint click could be heard under Stewart's touch, and they stepped back in surprise as a whole section of the wall receded.

'Bingo,' she murmured, and grabbed her torch.

A narrow landing lay on the opposite side of the opening leading to a flight of concrete steps that descended from the office level.

'All these old buildings down by the river were built with cellars,' said Stewart, peering over her shoulder. 'I remember reading about it once. That's what made me think of it.'

'Good work,' said Kay. She swung her torch down the stairwell.

Stale air wafted up to where they stood at the door opening, a strong scent tainted with body odour – and something else.

Something less tangible.

'What's that smell?' said Carys, her voice a notch higher.

'Fear,' said Kay. 'I think we found what we were looking for.'

# CHAPTER TWENTY-FIVE

Kay stepped back into the office and pulled her radio free.

'Guv? We've found something in the manager's office at the back of the building. Looks like the original cellar or something. It was concealed behind a hidden door. I'll have Stewart stay at the entrance to it in case it swings shut, but I'm taking Carys and Morrison with me to take a look.'

'Understood. On my way. Maintain radio contact, Hunter.'

'Will do.'

She signed off, then raised her chin so she could look Aaron Stewart in the eye. 'I reckon I'm going to struggle enough with the low ceiling down there if the other cellars I've seen around this town are anything to go by. You stay here and guide Inspector Sharp when he arrives, and keep that door open, you understand?'

'Sarge.'

She resisted the urge to shudder at the thought of being entombed below the nightclub if the door swung shut.

'Carys, Dave, you're with me. Stay alert. Single file. Carys, I want you in the middle, got that? No deviating from the path I set.'

'Got it.'

'Understood.'

Kay nodded. Thankfully, her colleagues were well experienced and she didn't have to explain that if they found evidence, then the ensuing crime scene investigation would be hampered by any of them not keeping to a strict path in and out of the cellar.

'All right, let's go.'

She shone her torch along the wall until she found a panel of switches, and pressed each one. To her relief, lights in the ceiling flickered to life, illuminating their way. She pushed her torch back into her belt, ignored the handrail set into the side of the wall, and made her way down the short flight of stairs.

She could hear Carys's breath as they descended, the younger detective's fear all too palpable, but she fought down the urge to turn back.

She had a job to do.

She paused at the bottom of the stairs, her heartbeat thudding in her ears.

Casting her eyes around the room, she saw that the basement area took up half of the above-ground space, and had been lined from floor to ceiling with large ceramic tiles.

A shudder passed through her body when she noticed the drain in the middle of the room, a past case flashing in her memory before she exhaled and discarded the thought.

As she raised her gaze, she fought the urge to flee.

Manacles had been set into the wall, dark stains covering the tiles below, aged and stubborn against removal.

She swallowed, then jumped at a tap on her shoulder.

'Sarge?'

She could hear the tremor in Carys's voice, but took a step forward, further into the room so her colleagues could follow.

She moved towards the back of the room, her eyes roaming over a steel table onto which a series of knives and other implements had been laid out as if by a craftsman proud of his work.

'Look.'

She turned at Morrison's voice, and looked to where he pointed, dread consuming her at the tone of his voice.

Blood splattered up the far corner of a wall, and the beam from Morrison's torch wavered as he shone it on the floor tiles.

A single tooth lay amongst a clump of hair.

'Enough.'

Kay spun on her heel and raced across the room, then up the narrow concrete staircase.

Sharp stood at the doorway to the cellar, his face troubled when she appeared, but she shook her head, unable to speak.

Instead, she pushed her way past him, leaving the office behind and staggering along the corridor to the chink of light that shone through the gap in the back door.

She shoved it open and stumbled into the alleyway, closing her eyes against the bright sunshine, her hands on her hips as she forced fresh air into her lungs.

Footsteps clattered behind her, and she turned around as Carys tumbled out through the door, her face pale.

The detective constable placed a gloved hand on the red brick wall of the empty Chinese takeaway shop and leaned over. She held up her other hand as Kay approached.

'I'm okay, I'm not going to be sick. I just—'

'Yeah. I know.'

Kay glanced over her shoulder as the back door slammed open once more on its broken hinges, and Sharp appeared.

He buttoned his suit jacket over his chest as he drew closer, and Kay noticed his hands shaking as he cast his eyes over the younger detective.

'You going to be all right, Miles?'

'Guv.'

'What about you, Hunter?'

His grey eyes swept over her, concern furrowing his forehead.

She took a deep breath, and exhaled slowly.

'Yeah. I'll be okay.'

'Sir, we found this a moment ago.'

They both turned at the sound of Morrison's voice, a quiver on the edges of his words as he strode towards them, his face grey.

He held up a wire, and Kay took it from him with shaking hands.

She recognised the blue colour all too well.

'It's an audio-visual cable – same as you'd use for your home entertainment system to connect it to speakers, or cameras,' he said.

*I know*, thought Kay. *He put them in my house, too.*

She handed it over to Sharp, their eyes locking.

He recognised it, too — thanks to his ex-military contacts, the microphones and miniature cameras she'd discovered in her house had been removed covertly, without alerting Demiri to the fact his surveillance had been thwarted. That recording equipment now sat hidden in a bank's safe deposit box to which only she and Sharp had keys.

'Looks like Demiri was filming what his clients were doing down here,' said Morrison.

'He gave himself some insurance, so they wouldn't talk about the place and betray him,' said Kay, turning the wire between her fingers. 'Jesus, what a monster.'

'Those poor women,' said Carys. 'All they wanted was a new life.'

'And this is how they paid for it. Hell of a way to go,' said Sharp, and visibly shivered. 'In all my years working on this team, I've never seen anything as bad as what's down here.'

Kay peered back at the nightclub. 'He's going to pay for this,' she snarled.

# CHAPTER TWENTY-SIX

Kay's mobile phone started ringing as she pushed her key into the front door lock and stumbled into the hallway.

Jostling the two shopping bags in her hand, she dropped her handbag onto the bottom stair tread, placed the bags at her feet and answered it a split second before it went to voicemail.

'Hi – how's it going?'

'You sound out of breath – everything okay?'

She could hear the note of panic in Adam's voice over the miles.

'I'm fine – you caught me as I was walking through the front door, that's all.' She moved her phone from one hand to the other as she shrugged off her jacket and placed it over the bannister before picking up the shopping bags and making her way through to the kitchen. 'So, what's it like?'

'Good, good. I'm really glad I came, to be honest.'

'There you go. If you'd stayed here, you'd have missed out. How did your presentation go?'

'Fantastic. I've made some more contacts – one of the chaps I got speaking with has a practice down in Devon I'll go and see next month—'

Kay let his voice wash over her, his enthusiasm and the normality of his words settling her after the trauma of the search at the nightclub. As she listened to him, she unpacked the bags, flipped the kettle on and settled at the worktop.

'What about you?'

His words jerked her from her relaxed state.

'Kay?'

'Sorry. I was thinking.'

She rubbed at her right eye, and sniffed.

'You all right?'

'Yeah. Tough day, that's all.'

'Well, I'm only sat here in an empty hotel bar all by myself with an average glass of Pinot Noir if you want to tell me about it?'

'No – no, that's okay. Thanks, though. Did you manage to catch up with that bloke you were hoping to meet?'

'Yes – he's picking me up from the hotel tomorrow morning so we'll be out for most of the day. I expect the mobile reception will be crap, too, so if you need me—'

'Really, everything's okay.' She smiled, letting warmth into her voice. 'You don't have to worry about me, promise.'

'You've got all the security lights on, yeah?'

'Yes.'

She proceeded to tell him about the visit from her colleagues the previous night, and he laughed.

'You'll never hear the end of it now.'

'You're right there. Thank goodness it's only four weeks until it's Gavin's turn to host us – they might have forgiven me by then.'

'How are Bonnie and Clyde?'

'Well, you'll be pleased to hear that Clyde's skin is healing well.'

'Oh, that is good news. I'll make a veterinary nurse out of you yet.'

'That's if they're still here when you get back. I think Carys has her eye on them.'

Laughter rang down the line. 'I might have known. What about work?'

They chatted for another twenty minutes, and then Adam mentioned his stomach was rumbling, so Kay shooed him off the call and promised to phone him the next night when he returned from his extended trip to the racing stables.

As she ended the call, a gust of wind blew against the kitchen window and she shuddered, glad it was he who would be braving the elements in the name of research, and not her.

# CHAPTER TWENTY-SEVEN

'Thought I'd find you here.'

Kay jerked upright, shaken from her thoughts, and turned her head to see Barnes approaching along the tow path towards her.

She moved her handbag and shuffled up the bench seat so he could join her, then turned her attention back to the line of narrowboats neatly moored along the opposite bank, mist rising from the water in the early morning sunlight.

He handed a Styrofoam cup to her.

'Coffee?'

'Spicy pumpkin soup. Marie at the café said it'd warm us up faster.'

'Thanks.'

She removed the plastic lid and blew across the hot surface of the liquid.

The tow path next to the River Medway had become a favourite haunt of Kay's over the summer months.

Tucked behind the grandeur of the Bishop's Palace, it provided a sanctuary from the bedlam of the police station and a respite from the noise of the café the team frequented.

Barnes had stumbled upon her there late one morning, and the two of them had spent time together since, mulling over various cases while devouring sandwiches or chatting over a quiet coffee.

'How're you doing this morning?' said Barnes. 'I heard, of course.'

'I'm okay,' said Kay. 'Frustrated and upset we didn't find out sooner. We might have saved some of them.'

'Can't play "what if", Sarge, you know that.'

'Yeah.'

'Are you going to tell me what's going on?'

Kay lowered the cup and turned her eyes to his. 'What do you mean?'

'Come on, Hunter. This is me you're talking to. How long have we known each other?'

'Too long.'

'Very funny. Look, I realise you probably didn't want to say anything front of Miles and Piper the other night, but come on. Something's troubling you.'

She sighed, and leaned back against the hard wooden planks of the seat, her gaze returning to the river and a pair of swans that glided past.

'I used to like this job, Ian. When I joined up, I thought I'd make a difference.' She choked out a bitter laugh. 'Now, I know that sounds naive, but it's true. That's why I worked so hard to make it to DS.

After the past eighteen months though, I'm beginning to wonder if I've made some sort of mistake.'

She sighed, and squinted up at the washed-out pale sky as a pair of jet trails stretched across the town, her thoughts turning to Adam.

The prospect of trips to the Continent with him excited her – they hadn't had a decent holiday in years, and if he could get some work on the conference circuit as he'd suggested, she'd be more than willing to tag along.

Barnes took a sip of soup, and then frowned. 'You're not quitting, are you?'

She shrugged in response.

''Cause if you did, it'd be a real shame. I know you're shaken up about what we found in that building – we all are. It's not a reason to get despondent about the number of criminals we're up against though.'

'It's not that, Ian – I mean, that was nasty, yes – it's the *politics* of everything. It's all the secrets and layers above us.'

He straightened, and shifted his weight so he could face her. 'Is this about Harrison?'

'I guess.'

'Because he's just like Larch, you know. Ambitious.'

'Speaking of ambitious – did you know about O'Reilly's secondment to SOCU before he appeared back here?'

'No – news to me. Mind you, we've always worked

on different teams here, so our paths haven't crossed, to be honest.'

Kay sipped her soup. 'Seems a strange choice, that's all. I never took him for a particularly good detective.'

'Oh?'

'Well, it's like that business with the attack on Gavin. It's gone nowhere.'

'In all fairness, Kay, you know how hard it is to get a result with attacks like that. No witnesses, and his attackers covered their faces.'

Kay shrugged, unwilling to concede the point. 'I'm still angry Harrison didn't come forward until now to tell us about his involvement though.'

'Think he did that on purpose?'

'Positioning himself to take over the case, you mean? Maybe.'

Barnes's eyes narrowed. 'I knew I didn't like him for a reason.'

'I suppose he has to protect his people. I can see it from his point of view.'

'Well, I'm glad you can. I guess you haven't lost that sense of ambition after all.'

Her jaw dropped open, and he winked.

'Be honest. You're not going to quit. Remember what you said to me after we found Emma that day? Take a break. Have a think about it.' He gestured to the swans paddling away from them and brushed his trousers down as he stood. 'But, I reckon you've done enough thinking for one day. Come on.'

He took her empty cup from her and tossed both into

a bin next to the tow path before turning back to her. 'What about what happened to you with the Professional Standards investigation? Are they going to do anything about it?'

Kay shook her head. 'I want Demiri, Ian. That's why I insisted Harrison let me onto his investigation. He couldn't really say no – they're understaffed as it is.'

Barnes emitted a low whistle, and shook his head.

'I hope you know what you're getting yourself into, Kay.'

# CHAPTER TWENTY-EIGHT

Kay cast her gaze over the people that filled the incident room.

Each and every one of them wore a grim expression; word had got around about what had been discovered within the bowels of Demiri's nightclub, and Kay knew what was troubling them.

Somehow, he'd managed to run his sick business without any of them knowing, and they had no idea how many women had been slaughtered before their bodies were dumped by Demiri's men.

Even O'Reilly seemed subdued, his normal bravado silenced by the scenes from the raid.

She watched as Gavin wandered over to Carys's desk, placed a steaming cup of coffee in front of her, and patted her shoulder.

Carys managed a smile, and the two of them spoke in hushed tones, bowed over their drinks.

Kay looked up as Sharp walked into the incident

room, a shorter man at his heels who wore a vexed expression and a receding hairline.

'Let's have your attention, everyone,' said Sharp as he passed the desks and headed towards the whiteboard at the end of the room.

Kay picked up her coffee mug and followed her colleagues.

Sharp paced the floor while they gathered, and then gestured to the other man.

'This is Colin Fox of the UK Border Agency,' he said. 'We've been meeting with DCI Harrison and the Chief Super about yesterday's events, and although Demiri appears to be in hiding at the present time, we're of the opinion that what he's been doing has been too lucrative for him to simply walk away. We also have Gareth Jenkins's assertion that Demiri was expecting another "shipment". In light of what was found yesterday at the nightclub, I think we can safely say that "shipment" refers to people, not drugs as was previously thought.'

Sharp continued to bring the rest of the investigation team up to date on what had been found.

'Of particular note is that the cellar hasn't been cleared of trace evidence – Harriet's team have plenty of forensic data they're compiling including fingerprints on some of the implements found.'

'Demiri?' said Kay, leaning forward in her seat.

'No. No trace of Jozef Demiri at all down there.'

'Leaving us clues to who his clients were, do you think, guv?' said Barnes.

'Quite possibly. Harriet and her team are still on site, and probably will be for some time yet,' he concluded. 'In the meantime, Colin has a separate team monitoring the Kent coastline for Demiri's boat. Colin, do you want to brief the team on your efforts to date?'

'Thanks, Sharp. We've had suspicions that Jozef Demiri has been smuggling people into the country via boat, but it's proven impossible to date to pinpoint exactly where the drop-offs occur. I believe some of you were involved in tracking movement of his fleet of trucks between here and the Continent, and that's certainly how we thought he was bringing in people to start off with.'

Kay raised her hand. 'Why haven't you been able to monitor incoming boats? Why have they been missed so far?'

'Detective, this county has three hundred and fifty miles of coastline. Our teams are constantly being redirected to support ongoing anti-terrorism efforts at Heathrow and the Channel Tunnel. Why do you think we missed them?'

Sharp cleared his throat. 'I think what Hunter meant was, how is Demiri managing to get these people into the country via the English Channel? It's a busy shipping lane, after all.'

Fox shrugged. 'He's running a very lucrative business. He can afford fast boats. They're small, too, so often we don't spot them. A lot of our successes to date in relation to people smuggling rely on tip-offs, or when the boats are in such a bad condition to start off with that they capsize before reaching land and the Coast Guard have to rescue the occupants. We have look-outs stationed along the coastline – we educate the local population and they help by reporting any unusual night-time activity. It's often the local fishermen who are our best assets. The problem is, Demiri and all the other people smugglers up and down the coast have their own lookouts.'

'So, you're up against people who are probably paying good money to the same informants you use and they look away?' said Barnes.

'Exactly.'

The room fell silent as the team began to gain an understanding of how hard Fox's role was, and why the Border Agency was under so much pressure.

Kay glanced over her shoulder as Harrison entered the room and stood next to O'Reilly, his arms crossed as he listened.

'You'd think knowing there's such a problem with migrants entering the country along the coastline, the government would recruit more people into the Border Agency,' said Carys.

'Maybe. Like I said, most of our resources have been relocated to cope with increases in immigration queues at Heathrow, though, so that's not always the answer.'

'What do you need from us?' said Sharp.

'Well, given your involvement from time to time with the joint Serious Crime Directorate, we could certainly use your assistance on this one. You know the locality, and any contacts you've got will help to add to the intelligence we've gathered to date.' Fox ran his hand over his hair. 'As it is, we're only going to get support from one Border Agency vessel.'

'One?' said Gavin. 'Surely they can provide more than one?'

Fox shook his head. 'Border Agency has five cutters. One of those is in dry dock for maintenance, one's down in the Mediterranean for the next three months, and I'm afraid we can't divert the other three without leaving other parts of the English coastline exposed to illegal vessels.'

Barnes emitted a low whistle. 'How many illegal boats do you catch?'

'Not enough. And we have no way of knowing how many we've missed. It doesn't help that we know a lot of French fishermen are exacerbating the influx by accepting bribes to bring people over the Channel.'

'I thought the Navy would be sent to the Mediterranean,' said Gavin.

'Budget cuts,' said Fox. 'And the government expects the Border Agency to make up the deficit.'

A collective groan passed through the incident room.

'In the meantime,' said Harrison, moving to the whiteboard, 'I've just heard from the Chief Super. We can't get any more staff support for our investigation, either, so we'll have to do the best with what we have.'

Sharp thanked Colin Fox, and led him from the room as Harrison worked his way around the detectives, seeking an update on their work.

Exasperated, he turned away from Carys. 'Does anybody have *anything* to progress this investigation?'

Gavin held up a sheaf of paperwork. 'Demiri's got more businesses, linked to his legitimate one, as subsidiaries to the main organisation.'

Harrison clicked his fingers and pointed at Gavin. 'Good point. He builds layers, so it makes it harder for us to investigate them. We've closed down some of them over the last two years, and there have been some convictions, but we've never got near Demiri himself. He's been too clever to get directly involved.'

Carys took one of the reports from Gavin, and ran her gaze down the page before wrinkling her nose.

'Garlic? He ran a business importing garlic?'

'One of the easiest ways to get illegal entrants into the country by road,' said Kay. 'Before everything happened eighteen months ago with the evidence going missing, we'd had some success arresting some men working for that garlic import business. They used to drive to the Continent once a month and come back with their van loaded with garlic for the French farmers' market in Lenham.'

She smiled at the look of confusion that swept across Carys and Gavin's faces. 'Garlic puts the sniffer dogs off the scent of people hiding in secret compartments built into the back of the vans. We only caught that lot because of a tip-off.'

'Like Fox said before, a lot of what we do is reliant on public vigilance,' said Sharp, returning to the front of the room and standing next to Harrison. 'Someone out there must know something to help us.'

Kay raised her hand to get his attention. 'Guv? If Demiri's been making snuff films of his clients' exploits, there might be another way we can find out where he might be. Those films had to be distributed for him to be making the sort of money we're talking about.'

Sharp frowned. 'Like what?'

'Not what. Who. Bob Rogers.'

# CHAPTER TWENTY-NINE

'Who the hell is Bob Rogers?'

Sharp closed his office door and gestured to the visitor chairs opposite his desk.

Kay sank into the least threadbare one, and bit back a smile as Harrison eased into the other, his lip curling at the lack of cushioning while he shuffled to try and find a comfortable seating position.

'Rogers was responsible for making snuff films of young girls,' said Sharp as he lifted a sheaf of paperwork off his chair and sat down, blatantly ignoring the sticky note marked "urgent" that had been placed on top of the documentation. He shoved the papers into a tray on the corner of his desk and loosened his tie. 'Kay was the assistant SIO on the case and helped put Rogers and his accomplice, Eli Matthews, behind bars for a long time.'

'What's he got to do with Demiri?'

'Rogers never told us who was distributing the snuff

films for him,' said Sharp. 'Eli didn't know – he was responsible for kidnapping the girls and arranging their deaths. Very elaborate in the case we were involved with. Rogers acted as middleman. Somewhere above him was the buyer and distributor.'

Harrison's brow furrowed. 'I remember hearing about that one now. Father and son, weren't they?'

'That's right.'

'My point is, for them to get away with it for so long without being caught meant Rogers had to be dealing with a highly sophisticated distribution network,' said Kay.

'One whose clientele would be willing to pay a lot of money to ensure anonymity,' said Sharp. 'And, like Kay said, Rogers wouldn't talk. We were never able to find a toehold into that distribution group.'

'Eli died in prison six months ago,' added Kay. 'He was attacked by two men and subsequently died of internal injuries four days later.'

'What happened to his attackers?'

'Charged with manslaughter and had their sentences extended,' said Sharp.

'Did they say why they attacked him?'

Sharp shrugged. 'The prison houses a lot of sex offenders. Despite that, attacks on young girls are still viewed as the worst, even within those walls and amongst those people. At the trial, when evidence was brought forward about Rogers' business history in Suffolk, it transpired that Eli's youngest victim was eight years old.'

'Where's Bob Rogers now?'

'Still here, in Maidstone Prison,' said Sharp.

Harrison beamed. 'Convenient.'

'We should talk to him as soon as possible,' said Kay, warming to her subject. 'Perhaps if we find a historical link between Rogers and the nightclub, we can use that to our advantage. He might give us some information about Demiri at last.'

'It's a long shot, but I agree we should talk to him. Make some phone calls this morning and see how fast a meeting can be set up. Tell them it's urgent. We need to talk to Rogers today,' said Harrison, wincing as he rose from his chair and straightened his trousers. 'It'll give him less time to prepare. I'll brief headquarters while you're doing that.'

Sharp's lips thinned, but he nodded.

Kay waited until the DCI had left the room, closing the door behind him with a soft *click*, and turned to Sharp.

'I'll make the call if you want.'

'Please. Despite what Harrison thinks, I've got better things to be doing than act as his secretary.' He gestured to the pile of paperwork waiting for him.

Kay grinned. 'He'll have you making cups of tea for him next.'

'Very funny. Clear off.'

# CHAPTER THIRTY

The smile she wore as she left Sharp's office left Kay's face as she walked back into the incident room and saw Gavin hurrying towards her, his face stricken.

'What's wrong?'

'Uniform have located another site.'

'Another site?'

'Three more women, dead. Asphyxiated.'

A chill swept across the back of her neck, a split second before she backtracked to Sharp's office.

'Guv? Gavin says uniform have found three more victims. Could be linked to Demiri?'

Sharp pushed his chair back. 'Gather everyone. No sense in Gavin repeating himself.'

A quick phone call roused Barnes and Carys from the canteen, both out of breath by the time they appeared in the incident room, the older detective dabbing his mouth with a napkin as he took a seat.

'Okay, Piper – bring us all up to speed, and then we'll sort out priorities,' said Sharp.

'Right, guv.' Gavin cleared his throat and then turned to his colleagues. 'A uniform patrol was assigned a call this morning from an elderly woman over at Thurnham. Said that there was a bad smell coming from a neighbouring property.'

'What made her call us, not environmental control over at the council?' said Barnes.

'She said she's tried phoning them before about issues with the tenant at the property leaving rubbish out and the like,' said Gavin. 'And she reported that in the past, she'd heard noises from the house – scuffles, muted voices, things like that. She thinks it's rented by a council tenant but apparently, there was something wrong with the plumbing and the council haven't got around to fixing it yet. She hasn't seen the tenant for a while, and was worried it was squatters.'

'Go on,' said Sharp.

'When uniform got there, they spoke to the woman first and ascertained she last heard the noises some three weeks ago. PC Norris says that he went around to the house, peered through the letterbox and immediately picked up the smell.'

He didn't need to elaborate.

All the team had been subjected to the stench of death at some point in their careers.

'When he broke down the door, he found the bodies of three women. He's requested an SIO attend, obviously and has the scene taped off while he's waiting for Harriet and her team to get there.'

'All right, thanks Gavin,' said Sharp. 'Kay – you're with me. Go get a pool car ready to leave in five minutes. Barnes, Carys – work with uniform and have them start on the house-to-house enquiries while you speak to Mrs—'

'Evans,' said Gavin.

'Thanks. Debbie – get on to the council and request a list of tenants and anyone else who has access to a key to that house. Including council employees, work contractors, the lot. Let's go.'

He clapped his hands together, and the team sprang into action, Kay grabbing her jacket and leading the way down to the car park.

Sharp pulled his mobile phone from his jacket pocket as she pointed the car in the direction of Thurnham, and she caught a glimpse of Harrison's number on the display before turning her attention to the traffic around her.

'Harrison? Where are you at the moment?'

A muffled response was all Kay heard, before Sharp spoke once more, passing on the details of the property they were heading towards.

'Understood.' He finished the call and tucked the phone into his jacket pocket. 'Harrison's going to be at headquarters for a while yet. He's happy for us to attend, with a view to getting an update at the afternoon briefing.'

They remained silent the rest of the way, Kay

concentrating on her driving while trying to manoeuvre the car through the traffic as quickly as possible.

Reaching the outskirts of the urban sprawl, she pressed the accelerator and expertly steered the vehicle around narrow countryside lanes.

As she turned into the road leading to the address provided by uniform, she realised why the location would have been perfect for Demiri's purposes.

A single winding lane revealed only two properties. Two patrol cars were parked outside the first on the right-hand side of the road, the vehicle's occupants already busy talking to an older woman who stood between the vehicles, her arms crossed over her chest.

Kay slowed as she drew near, then wound down her window.

One of the uniformed officers hurried towards her and bent down until he was level with her. He nodded to Sharp in the passenger seat, and then pointed up the road.

'The crime scene is up there, just over the crest of the hill. There are two more cars there, and we've got the area taped off.'

Kay's eyes drifted to the woman. 'Is she the one that called in?'

'Yes. She was walking her dog earlier this morning. The wind direction must have changed as she passed her neighbours' house, because she said she hadn't noticed it before even though she walks the dog the same way every morning. Apparently, she went up to the front door and knocked but didn't expect anybody to answer, because she said the last time she knew someone was actually living there was over a year ago. She tried to look through the windows, but couldn't see anything. She says she doesn't know why, but she just felt that something wasn't right and that's why she called us.'

'Okay, thanks.'

He stepped back from the car and Kay checked her mirror before pulling back into the lane.

Within seconds, they could see the second property and two more patrol cars parked outside.

The wind buffeted Kay as she stepped from the vehicle, and she cast her gaze over the low hedge opposite the property that separated the lane from a fallow field.

Grey clouds billowed across the sky, giving the landscape an oppressive atmosphere.

She shivered as she turned back to the house, a bright holly bush sprawling across the front of the building a stark contrast to the horror she knew she'd find within.

'Ready?'

Sharp's words jolted her from her thoughts.

'Yes. Let's take a look.'

She opened the back door of the car and pulled out two sets of coveralls, handing one to Sharp and then slipping her set over her blouse and trousers before tying plastic booties over her shoes.

As she straightened, PC Norris approached, his eyes troubled.

'Inspector Sharp?'

'Yes, and this is DS Hunter, who I think you already know. You were first on the scene?'

'I had to break the door down – the neighbour down the road didn't have a key, and there was no answer when we knocked,' said Norris. 'In the circumstances, I took the decision we need to get in there as quickly as possible. The crime scene has been preserved, and I've made a note of any surfaces I may have touched. A pathologist has been requested and should be here soon to declare life extinct.'

'Okay,' said Sharp. 'We understand there are three victims?'

'That's right. We searched the rest of the house, as well as an old shed out the back, but there are no more bodies. The property doesn't have a cellar, either.'

'Okay. Lead the way.'

Kay followed the two men, and wondered what horrors had been left for them this time.

# CHAPTER THIRTY-ONE

Kay was immediately struck by the stench of death. She began to take shallow breaths through her mouth, trying to avoid breathing through her nose and inhaling the smell that filled the property.

'They're through here.' Norris approached a door and stood to one side.

Kay watched as Sharp stood on the threshold of the room and peered in.

After a moment, he turned to her. 'They've been here a while.'

Kay swallowed and stepped forward. 'How did we miss this, guv?'

'He's clever, Hunter. And he has a whole network of people working for him, and protecting him.'

Kay folded her arms over her chest, then followed Sharp as he began to circle the room.

Bare, except for three wooden chairs arranged to face each other in the centre of the room, the space reflected no light from outside, the single window covered by net curtains and grime.

On each of the three chairs, a dead woman sat.

Each woman had had a plastic bag placed over her head, arms tied behind her and her hands fastened to the back of the chair.

Flies swarmed in the air, and Kay waved her hand in front of her face as one of the insects came too close.

Her brow furrowed as her gaze ran over the space in the middle of the three chairs.

Each woman had been placed so she could see the previous victim, only increasing the terror she must have endured in her final moments.

Kay averted her eyes as a maggot dropped to the floor from one of the victim's bodies, and fought down the urge to flee.

'How long have they been here, do you think?'

'Several weeks, I'd guess,' said Sharp. 'Except for this one.'

He dropped to a crouch as he approached the woman with her back to the door, her head at an impossible angle to her shoulder. His brow creased.

'What is it?' Kay drew nearer.

'We'll have to get Lucas to confirm during the post mortem, but I don't think she died from asphyxiation – look.'

Kay held her breath and bent closer to where Sharp squatted, and looked to where he pointed.

A large hole could be seen in the plastic near the woman's mouth.

'She bit it?'

'That's what I think. And I think someone broke her neck instead.'

He straightened and swept imaginary dust from his trousers.

Kay's eyes swept the other two bodies.

The plastic bags had protected the women's faces from being ravaged by nature, their terrifying final moments locked forever in milky eyes.

'Do you think it's Demiri?'

In response, Sharp pointed to the three marks in the dust on the floor in the middle of the chairs. 'Those look like the sort of marks a camera tripod would leave. So, yes, I think he – or at least someone working for him – filmed these women's last moments. We'll know for sure once Harriet and her team have been through here and Lucas has done the post mortem, but it'd be one hell of a coincidence if it wasn't, don't you think?'

Kay muttered a noncommittal response, keen not to inhale any more of the fetid air than was absolutely necessary.

Sharp completed his circuit of the room, ran his eyes over the three victims once more, and then jerked his head towards the door.

'Come on. We don't want to contaminate this scene any more than necessary.'

He stopped abruptly in the hallway as Lucas Anderson, Home Office pathologist, entered the house.

'Sorry I'm late,' he said, his face harried. 'Traffic on the M26.'

Sharp shrugged. 'It won't take you long to declare death.'

He pushed past the pathologist and out into the front garden of the house.

Lucas raised an eyebrow at Kay, and she shrugged.

'It's a bad one,' she said. 'He's taking this personally.'

The pathologist checked over his shoulder, before turning back to her. 'Keep an eye on him, Hunter. I've heard he's been under a lot of pressure lately.'

Kay frowned, but nodded as Lucas patted her arm and moved past her, then hurried after her DI.

She found him on the opposite side of the lane by the time she'd discarded her protective overalls in the bin the forensic team had set up upon their arrival.

He stood with his hands shoved in his pockets, gazing up at the house.

'Seems to me that Demiri is getting sloppy in his panic to leave the area,' he said as she drew near.

'I don't think it's as simple as that, guv.' She shivered as she followed his gaze, and watched as the forensic team stopped on the threshold to talk with Lucas. 'To me, it's almost as if he's leaving a trail of breadcrumbs.'

# CHAPTER THIRTY-TWO

A subdued atmosphere hung over the afternoon briefing, news of the full horror of the discovery at the abandoned smallholding reaching the investigation team before Kay and Sharp had returned.

Harrison stuck his head out from Sharp's office, his manner one of efficiency as soon as he saw them.

'Right, let's rally the troops.' He disappeared back into the room, the sound of a filing cabinet door being slammed shut filling the void.

Sharp winced.

'Okay, guv?'

'He wasn't even in the bloody army,' he muttered, and stormed towards his open office door.

Kay shrugged and crossed the room to the water cooler, swallowing her drink in three large gulps before making her way to her desk and dropping her bag to the floor.

'You've got a face like thunder,' said Barnes from the desk opposite hers.

She glanced over her shoulder to check their senior officers were out of earshot, then back to Barnes.

'Something's going on with Sharp,' she said. 'I've never known him like this. Even Lucas said he'd noticed he seemed under pressure at the moment.'

'Hits us all sometime.'

'Maybe.'

'Perhaps he's feeling a bit threatened by Harrison sharing the investigation, do you think?'

'Yeah. Could be.' She jerked her chin towards the office. 'What's he been doing while we were out?'

Barnes grinned. 'He only turned up an hour ago – some sort of meeting over at HQ. Plenty of pep talk about teamwork when he got back. All hot air, of course. I think he's been checking the files to see if there are any easy ones he can solve to make Sharp look bad.'

'Bastard. I knew he couldn't be trusted.'

They broke off their conversation at the sound of a low whistle from the direction of the whiteboard.

Sharp stood next to Harrison, his eyes blazing.

'Shall we start this briefing, ladies and gentlemen? We have a lot to work through.'

The team scurried to the far end of the incident room, grabbing chairs or perching on the ends of desks before extracting notebooks. Eventually, the noise died down.

'Debbie – how did you get on with finding out who owns the property?'

'The last tenants the council has on record left eighteen months ago, guv. Since then, they've had workers go around and check the building – water leaks, security, that sort of thing. Apparently, that hasn't happened for about six months though – lack of resources, they told me.'

'Did they give you a note of the last person to attend site?'

'Yes, and a mobile number for him. Paul Robinson. He's agreed to be interviewed at three o'clock, when he finishes his shift.'

Sharp checked his watch. 'In half an hour. Great work, Debbie. Anything else?'

'There have been no reports to the council about stolen keys or any issues since the last tenants left. The property was simply abandoned. I'm waiting to hear back from the council with details of the last tenants, and I'll follow that up.'

'Okay. Piper, Miles – I'd like you to do the interview with Robinson. If he hasn't been there for six months, I don't expect much, but find out if he noticed anything untoward.'

'Guv,' said Carys. Her pen hovered over her notebook. 'Do you think he might have gone back in the interim – you know, out of curiosity?'

'Great idea,' said O'Reilly. 'Brilliant – it's definitely worth asking, Miles. He could be a suspect.'

'We'll make a SOCU detective out of you yet, Carys,' said Harrison.

Sharp cleared his throat, before consulting the notes in his hand. 'Right, since Hunter and I returned, Harriet has phoned with her preliminary findings. As we suspected, two of the victims had been there for at least a month, given the state of decomposition. The third victim may have been there for only a couple of weeks – Lucas will confirm that in due course. Of note was the fact that the third victim managed to bite through the plastic, and so didn't die from asphyxiation. Instead, her neck had been broken. Hunter – CSI have also confirmed that the markings we saw on the floor do resemble those from a camera tripod, so we can assume each victim's death was filmed.'

'If the third victim had her neck broken, then her killer must've been on camera,' said Kay.

A shocked silence filled the room.

'If we can locate the film, then we might be able to identify her killer,' said Harrison. 'Although I'd be surprised if he didn't have his face covered.'

'It's worth pursuing though – good point, Hunter,' said Sharp.

He glared as the phone in his office began to ring, and pointed at Debbie. 'West, get that and if it's not urgent grab a number and call them back.'

'Guv.'

He turned his attention to the three photographs now pinned to the whiteboard, their grim portrayals of the three victims all too clear. 'As soon as Harriet and her team have fingerprints and any other information about these three women available, I want them identified.'

'What if they're illegal entrants?' said Barnes, voicing Kay's own concerns.

Sharp sighed, and ran a hand through his hair. 'We'll do our best for them, is that understood?'

'Guv,' the team murmured as one.

'Inspector?'

All eyes fell to Debbie as she emerged from Sharp's office, her eyes wide.

'What is it, West?'

'That was Governor Bagley over at the prison,' said Debbie. 'Bob Rogers has been attacked.'

# CHAPTER THIRTY-THREE

Kay shrugged her jacket over her shoulders and hurried after Sharp, ignoring the glare from Harrison as he watched them leave.

She had no idea why he and Sharp seemed to be at loggerheads recently, but it seemed to stem from the meeting he said he'd been having at headquarters.

If she were honest, she didn't care. All she cared about was ensuring they arrested Demiri as soon as possible. She had no time for the politics surrounding the case.

Sharp stomped down the stairs ahead of her, not waiting to see if she was keeping up. She caught the eye of a uniformed sergeant as Sharp stormed past, and he raised an eyebrow.

She shook her head.

Now wasn't the time for humour, or an explanation.

Instead, she hurried to catch up with the detective inspector, holding her hand out to stop the back door to the police station closing in her face. By the time she'd left the building, he was already starting the car, his black mood etched across his face.

She climbed into the passenger seat and fastened her belt as he accelerated out the car park.

The prison was only a mile or so away from the police station as the crow flies, but thanks to 1960s civil engineering, they had to travel a convoluted route around the ring road to reach it.

Over two hundred years old, the prison housed around six hundred inmates, many of whom were sex offenders. A dark coloured Kentish ragstone brick wall surrounded the prison buildings, obscuring them from public view.

Despite the numerous awards the inmates had won for their gardening efforts, Kay felt repulsed at the undue attention it gave the prison. As far she was concerned, they were there as punishment, and not for recreation, and she didn't believe any of them could be rehabilitated back into society.

She battened down her thoughts as the car drew to a standstill at the gatehouse, and checked the notes she'd printed out when she'd first suggested they speak with Bob Rogers.

The prison comprised four residential buildings for inmates, however for his own safety Bob Rogers had been sent to the segregation unit.

Kay snorted at the irony.

'Did you say something?'

'No, guv. Reading the notes, that's all.'

Sharp grunted a reply, and wound down his window as a guard approached.

'You'll need to move your car over.'

'What?'

The guard jerked a thumb over his shoulder. 'Ambulance is on its way out. You're blocking the way.'

Sharp swore under his breath, shoved the car into reverse and swung his arm over the back of Kay's seat as he manoeuvred the vehicle back onto the narrow street that ran in a parallel line to the prison walls. Terraced houses faced the prison, and parked cars lined the road.

'Can't see a bloody thing,' he muttered as he craned his neck.

Kay twisted in her seat. 'Clear.'

Sharp reversed the car into the road, and then sat quietly fuming while he drummed his fingers on the steering wheel.

Kay straightened as an ambulance shot through the gates and tore down the street beyond their position, its siren blaring and lights ablaze.

'That doesn't look good,' she said.

Sharp cranked the car into first gear. 'I've got a bad feeling about this, too.'

Once through the gates, the guard now pacified that the ambulance had been able to leave swiftly, Sharp swung the car into a space and they made their way to the entrance to the prison.

A small crowd had convened at the next set of gates,

and Kay recognised a mid-set man amongst them as the governor.

He didn't look like he was having a good day.

He raised his eyes from the man he'd been deep in conversation with – a guard with blood down the front of his shirt – and waved them over.

'Go and get cleaned up, Perkins. A job well done, by the way. You did all you could.'

Kay watched the prison guard disappear into a building off to the left, then turned her attention back to the governor.

'Mr Bagley,' she said, shaking his hand after Sharp.

'Detectives.' He ran a hand over his tie and smoothed it down, an almost unconscious movement as his eyes tracked the forecourt.

'What happened?' said Sharp.

'Rogers was set upon by a man armed with a screwdriver. Stab wounds to the chest and abdomen.' He jerked his thumb over his shoulder. 'Perkins was first on scene with a colleague of his. They restrained the attacker, and then Perkins did his best to stabilise Rogers while we waited for the ambulance.'

'How bad is it?'

The governor's eyes looked troubled. 'Bad, I'm afraid. The ambulance took over twenty minutes to get here – school traffic, you see. By the time they arrived, Rogers had already lost a lot of blood.'

'What about his attacker?' said Kay.

The man shook his head. 'He's refusing to talk. There'll be a full investigation, obviously.'

Sharp pursed his lips. 'A shame we couldn't get an appointment to speak with him sooner.'

Bagley's brow furrowed. 'Detective Inspector, my team's first priority is the wellbeing of our prisoners. We can't upset the whole prison routine simply because you decide you want to speak to one of them. Arrangements have to be made, and the prisoner informed of your wishes.'

Sharp held up his hands. 'Sorry. Frustrating, that's all.'

Bagley nodded. 'Understood.'

'Who else knew we were planning to speak to Rogers?' said Kay.

'Myself and half a dozen members of staff,' said Bagley. 'Plus Rogers, of course, and whoever he might've told.'

Kay glanced down as her bag started to vibrate, a moment before her phone began to ring.

'Excuse me,' she said. 'I need to take this.'

She took a few paces away from Sharp and Bagley, then answered. 'What's up, Barnes?'

'We just received a call from the hospital,' said the older detective, his voice resigned. 'Bob Rogers didn't make it. Dead on arrival.'

'Shit,' Kay murmured, then, 'thanks.'

Ending the call, she made her way back to the two men and passed on the news.

'I can't say I'm surprised,' said Bagley. 'He wasn't in a good way when he left here.'

Sharp sighed, and held out his hand to the governor.

'Let us know what you manage to find out. I'll keep in touch, and if our investigation throws any light on why this happened, I'll let you know.'

'Likewise,' said Bagley.

Kay followed Sharp back to the car, both of them lost in thought until they reached the vehicle.

'Demiri found out, didn't he?' she said.

'Or, he pre-empted us.'

'Tidying up loose ends, you think?'

Sharp placed his hands on the top of the car and turned his head to the prison entrance behind them. 'That's what worries me, Hunter. What if he takes this boatload of people and runs? Sets up somewhere else? We'll have lost every advantage we had.'

Kay grimaced. She didn't say it out loud, but right now she couldn't recall one single advantage they'd had in the first place.

# CHAPTER THIRTY-FOUR

Kay adjusted the volume on her headphones before hitting the "play" button on the video once more.

On her computer screen the recorded video of Paul Robinson, the last council worker to visit the smallholding at Thurnham, was playing; Gavin and Carys sat opposite the man in an interview room as he told them about his last visit.

'It was nothing, really,' he said, his voice sounding reedy over the recording equipment. 'One of the property owners further up the lane made a complaint about the number of rubbish bags left outside the property – worried about rats, she said.'

'What happened when you got there?' said Carys.

'There was no-one in, so I made arrangements for the bags to be picked up on the next rubbish collection the following Monday, and issued a notice to the tenant to be sure to keep the place tidy and free from vermin.'

'Isn't it unusual to have properties like this on your books?'

The man shrugged. 'Not really. Some of the buildings like this used to belong to different departments for different reasons over the years. That house used to belong to the environmental department, for instance. As the council has had to reduce its budgets in different areas over the years, the buildings have been rented out. Brings in an income, you see.'

'What about references for the tenants of this one, or forwarding addresses?' said Gavin.

Robinson leaned back in his chair, and held up his hands. 'For some reason, the last record we've got for that place is for an older woman by the name of Mrs Boyston. I did some checking before I came here. It seems that, ah, she died fourteen months ago.'

'Fourteen months ago?' said Carys.

'We're understaffed, like I said. Budget cuts. Look, the rent kept being paid on time, so the council had no reason to question the tenancy.'

'But surely the death certificate would have been sent to you?'

'It seems to have been mislaid.'

Kay groaned, and pulled her headphones from her ears, then reached out and stopped the recording.

She logged out of the system, switched off her computer and swung her bag over her shoulder.

The incident room had emptied half an hour ago, a subdued air hanging amongst the team as the news of Bob Rogers' death had reached them.

Despite the temptation to grab a takeaway on the way home for convenience, she changed her mind when she realised the guinea pigs had been eating a healthier diet than her in Adam's absence from the house.

Twenty minutes later, she pulled into her driveway, determined to use up the bag of salad in the refrigerator before it started to sprout a whole new species, and consoled herself with the fact that at least she had at least two glasses of white burgundy left in a bottle to wash it down with.

After feeding Bonnie and Clyde and then herself, she sat at the kitchen worktop, a manila file open at her elbow filled with her own notes about the investigation while she drew a series of linking circles, all connected to one name.

*Jozef Demiri.*

She dropped the pen and took a sip of wine. Everything pointed to Demiri retreating from his business ventures, perhaps even from the southern coast of England, and she simply couldn't afford to let him escape.

Her thoughts returned to Harrison and O'Reilly.

Would Harrison let her have a chance to be the one to arrest Demiri when the time came, or would he seize the opportunity for himself? Would he ensure O'Reilly was the one to accompany him rather than see anyone from Sharp's team take the credit?

She set down her wine glass, determined that whatever happened politically between her two senior officers, she'd be present to see the Albanian people smuggler's face when he was charged with the murder of Katya and the other victims.

Her mobile vibrated on the worktop a second before it started to ring, and she reached across for it, recognising her sister's phone number.

'Hi, Abby.'

'Hang on.'

Kay rolled her eyes as her sister attempted to cover the phone before her muffled voice reached her ears, berating the eldest of her two toddlers and then returning, breathless.

'Honestly, those two. I swear I'm going to get an egg timer set up when they're playing so they share the toys fairly.'

'Like Mum did with us, you mean?'

'Worked, didn't it?'

They both laughed at the memory.

'I hadn't heard from you for a while. Everything okay?' said Abby.

After months of silence, Kay had finally confided in her family about the miscarriage triggered by the Professional Standards investigation she'd been subjected to.

Her work colleagues had found out by accident; a rumour spread around the police station thanks to a series of listening devices placed in her house. Kay suspected Jozef Demiri – or at least one of his lackeys – of the handiwork and subsequent tip-off to try to fracture the team around her, but she still had no proof and, rather than have them find out by other means like her colleagues, she'd taken the decision to tell her family one summer afternoon she and Adam had been at her parents' house for a barbeque.

It hadn't gone down well.

'You there?'

'Sorry.' Kay took another sip of wine. 'I'm fine. Busy at work, as usual. Adam's up in Aberdeen at a conference all week. How are things with you?'

She smiled as her sister carried on about Emily's antics at her daily play group, and then tuned out as the topic turned to the baby, Charlotte, and the perils of potty training.

'Aren't you going to ask how Mum is?'

'Did she ask after me?'

Kay's mother had been furious when she'd finally been told about Kay's miscarriage – both at being kept in the dark about the news, but also at Kay for taking her career so seriously that she'd endangered the life of her grandchild.

Shocked at her mother's selfishness, and disappointed at herself for not realising that her mother's reaction had been predictable given her previous lack of support for whatever Kay did with her life, Kay had stormed from the house leaving Adam to make their excuses for leaving while she fumed in the car.

Her father had been devastated.

He'd phoned the following Tuesday morning, their usual time to chat while her mother was out of the house, and both of them had ended the call in tears.

She hadn't spoken to her mother since the barbeque.

'No, she didn't ask after you.'

Kay sighed. 'Sorry you got dragged into this. I didn't mean for it to happen.'

She could almost hear the shrug at the end of the phone.

'S'okay. She'll come around.'

'Eventually.'

They both said the word at the same time, and Abby managed a small laugh.

'I've got to go, sis. Big day tomorrow,' said Kay.

'Okay. Love you.'

'Love you, too.'

Kay ended the call, slid the phone across the worktop, and picked up the photograph showing her quarry leaving his offices some six months before.

'I'd rather take on *you* any day compared to my family, Demiri.'

# CHAPTER THIRTY-FIVE

'Settle down.'

Harrison stalked to the front of the incident room, and paced in front of the whiteboard while Kay and her colleagues stopped talking and faced the detective chief inspector.

Sharp leaned against a desk to one side of the room, his eyes sweeping over the assembled uniformed officers and detectives as they found seats or somewhere else to perch and a silence descended, save for the scratch of pens on paper.

'Right. First of all, thanks to you all for the early start. I appreciate it's no fun being at work at sparrow's fart, but I'm sure you appreciate the importance of striking Demiri now.'

Harrison held up two documents in his right hand. 'These are the warrants we were seeking to search both his offices in Ashford and his house. Debbie, love, can you dim the lights?'

Kay caught Gavin's expression at the term of endearment and gave him a slight shake of her head.

Harrison's management techniques belonged in the Dark Ages, but now wasn't the time to debate it.

As she turned back, she saw O'Reilly bend down from his position on the corner of Carys's desk and whisper something to the detective constable. Carys covered her mouth with her hand and responded, her eyes never leaving Harrison, but Kay saw the wink that O'Reilly gave her before turning his attention to the front of the room.

'At this rate, we'll be losing even more people to SOCU,' she grumbled under her breath. 'Including the Jake O'Reilly fan club.'

'What was that?' Gavin hissed next to her.

'Nothing.'

'Right.' Harrison's voice cut across the room, and tapped the image on the whiteboard. 'Floor plans for Demiri's offices.'

Kay turned her attention to the DCI as he extolled Carys's attempts to get copies of the building's layout from the council's planning department, and wondered why he hadn't sought assistance from their colleagues in Ashford.

She nibbled at the end of her pen as she listened, and then realised Harrison was so determined that Demiri be arrested by his investigation team, he was likely leaving as many people out of the loop as possible to protect his position.

It worried her, and despite his assertions as the

briefing continued that they'd have support from a local uniform contingent when conducting the raid, she wondered what the ramifications might be when the detectives there found out they'd been snubbed.

She scribbled a note to herself as the image flickered and a new one appeared, that of an aerial photograph of a large sprawling house surrounded by woodland.

Harrison grinned, his face illuminated in a grotesque mask in the light from the overhead projector.

'We haven't been as lucky with Demiri's house,' he said. 'For those of you joining us today and who aren't aware, this property is on the outskirts of Pluckley.'

He flicked the switch and another image appeared. 'This photograph was taken this morning by SOCU officers monitoring the property some distance away. You can see here that there appears to be three entrances – front door, back door next to what we believe to be a kitchen, and these double doors onto the paved patio that leads into the garden. I want officers at all entrances prior to us going in. Currently intelligence from previous reports by Gareth Jenkins suggests that Demiri has at least four live-in staff, and a number of people visiting his house on a day-to-day basis, so we need to make sure we restrain anyone trying to leave in a hurry. D'you want to get your team up to speed, Sharp?'

The DI nodded, and made his way to the front of the room. 'I want two teams accompanying uniform, so Piper and Miles – you're leading the search of Demiri's offices. Barnes – I want you at the house. That way, we can have a high level debrief the moment you're back here rather than wait for reports to be updated onto the system.'

He held up his hand for silence as a murmur swept the room, the team's impatience palpable. 'I don't need to tell you how dangerous Demiri and his men are, or how important these searches are to our investigation, so watch out for each other, and get the job done properly.'

He handed the meeting back to Harrison who concluded by echoing Sharp's order for restraint before dismissing the team.

Kay turned at O'Reilly's voice as he passed her desk.

'Miles? Be careful, yeah?'

Carys's eyes opened wide at O'Reilly's words, but she nodded. 'Of course, Sarge. Always.'

'Obviously hasn't heard about you taking on a moving train,' mumbled Gavin as he followed her out the room.

Kay could hear them still bickering as the door swung shut behind them, and smiled to herself.

At least Gavin could be trusted to keep Carys's mind on the job and not the detective sergeant during the raid.

'O'Reilly?'

'Guv?'

'A word in Sharp's office. Got a special task for you.' Harrison beamed, and gestured towards the open door.

Kay stayed in her seat as the overhead lights sprang

back to life, and stared at the fading image of the house as the projector was switched off.

Why hadn't she been included in one of the search teams?

# CHAPTER THIRTY-SIX

Kay rubbed her eye and strained her ears to listen to the rapid fire orders being barked over the radio.

Debbie set down a mug of tea in front of her, then hovered at the end of the desk.

'Has it started yet?'

'No. They're waiting for the order to go in.'

'Bet you wish you were there,' said Debbie, before returning to her own side of the incident room.

Kay's thoughts turned to the cellar they'd discovered beneath Demiri's nightclub, and shuddered. She said nothing, and instead leaned across the pile of paperwork in front of her and turned up the volume on the radio.

The door to Sharp's office was wrenched open, and Harrison appeared, his whole body exuding tension.

'Are they ready?'

'Yes, guv. Waiting for your order,' said Kay, and handed him the radio. 'HQ are ready, too. They've got patrol cars set up to block access in and out of the road on the industrial park where Demiri's offices are, as well as the road outside his house.'

'Good.' Harrison glanced over his shoulder as Sharp strode towards them, his tie askew.

Kay frowned, then turned away.

His face appeared thunderous, and she'd never seen him with a tie that wasn't knotted and perfectly straight.

She wondered what Harrison had said to him behind closed doors that had him so riled, then pushed the thought away as Harrison raised the radio.

'All teams, this is DCI Harrison. You have a "go" for Operation Exodus. Repeat, Operation Exodus is a "go".'

Kay groaned inwardly at the call sign that had been randomly designated to the search operation, and crossed her fingers in the hope it wasn't an omen.

Harrison replaced the radio on the desk in front of Kay and turned to Sharp.

'Let's hope your team perform well. Can't have them slowing down SOCU, after all.'

A muscle worked in Sharp's jaw. 'They're all good officers, Simon, and more than capable of the job in hand. Same as they were when we raided the nightclub.'

Harrison sniffed. 'We'll see. What do you think, Hunter? Reckon we'll finally net Demiri after all this time?'

'Hope so, guv.'

'Shame we had to keep you here, really,' he said. 'I wouldn't have minded seeing Demiri's face when you turned up at his house.'

Kay's eyes travelled across to Sharp once more.

The DI was standing with his hands in his pockets, contemplating the carpet.

'Not a problem, guv,' she said to Harrison, injecting more warmth into her words than she felt. 'At least we'll be able to filter all the information as it comes through and develop a strategic approach to questioning him as the searches continue.'

Harrison beamed. 'You're quite right, Hunter. Commendable thinking.'

He turned his attention to a uniformed police officer who approached them and ran his signature over a series of forms before dismissing the man, and then made his way across to the whiteboard and stood in front of it, hands on hips, apparently lost in thought.

Sharp sank into the chair next to hers and leaned forward, elbows on knees as they listened to the chatter over the airwaves.

Both searches were being coordinated through the communications team at HQ where, much to his obvious disgust, DS O'Reilly had been sent by Harrison to monitor progress and provide him with immediate access to the team coordinator if he needed to send an urgent message.

'I should be out in the field,' he'd grumbled to Kay on his way out the door.

Kay had smiled sweetly, but had had the sense to keep quiet.

'The vest cameras from Piper and Miles are live,'

Debbie called over from her desk. 'I've emailed you a link to the feed.'

Kay opened her emails and clicked on the link, and took a sip of tea while the screen loaded.

'At last,' Sharp muttered as the images flickered to life.

The live video recording from Gavin's camera had sound, but Kay turned it down in favour of listening to O'Reilly's commentary over the radio.

Team one were responsible for the raid on Demiri's offices, while the second team had been tasked with his house.

Timed to precision, both teams converged on each of the properties within seconds of each other.

Kay watched as Gavin's camera picked up the tactical response team hovering at the fringes of the gathered response vehicles, before he approached the front doors of the industrial unit.

She inhaled sharply as he placed his hand on the front door and it swung inwards.

'Unlocked?'

'Not a good sign,' said Sharp.

Harrison spun away from the whiteboard. 'What's wrong?'

Sharp pointed at the video feed. 'When we interviewed Demiri at his offices, the doors were locked and we had to wait to be admitted. There was a video camera above the door and an intercom system.'

Harrison rubbed his chin. 'He's probably expecting us, and couldn't be bothered with the security charade.'

Kay caught the look that Sharp threw at Harrison and raised her eyebrow, but her DI gave a slight shake of his head and turned his attention back to the screen.

The black and white image wobbled slightly as Gavin moved through the door and held it open for Carys. Kay caught a flash of Carys's face, the woman's expression determined, and then the angle swung back to the reception area she and Sharp had entered only days before.

She frowned. 'Guv? Where's the reception desk?'

Sharp shook his head, his eyes never leaving the images on the screen.

On the radio, Gavin's voice rang out, confirming her fears.

'Looks like the place has been deserted.'

Harrison snatched the radio from the desk. 'Piper – check the conference room off to the left.'

Kay held her breath as Gavin's camera panned round and then began moving towards the large meeting room she and Sharp had been shown to by Demiri.

The door swung open, revealing a large empty space where the conference table had once been, and a darker rectangle against the far wall where the large flat screen television had once hung.

Harrison swore under his breath, then pulled his mobile phone from his pocket. 'O'Reilly? Demiri's offices are empty. What's the status from the team at the house?'

Kay watched as the DCI's face reddened, his eyes

blazing at the image on the screen in front of him, before he ended the call.

'Barnes has confirmed Demiri's house has also been abandoned,' he said, his voice dangerously low. He picked up the radio once more. 'Piper – clear the building. Lock it down for forensics immediately.'

'Understood, guv.'

'He's shut down all his operations, hasn't he?' said Kay. 'He's on the run.'

Next to her, Sharp slumped in his chair and ran a hand over his face.

Harrison handed Kay the radio, stormed away from her desk, then stalked into Sharp's office and slammed the door with enough force to shake the windows.

# CHAPTER THIRTY-SEVEN

Jozef Demiri stood with his back to the room, his eyes travelling over the landscape before him.

A smile twitched at the corner of his mouth, but he knew he couldn't relax.

Not yet.

However, it was too easy to imagine the reaction of the police when they discovered he'd outwitted them, and he wished he could see their faces when they discovered both his offices and home empty and devoid of any evidence.

He tugged at a loose thread on the woollen sweater he wore over a long-sleeved t-shirt and jeans, common clothing that he hadn't worn in years in favour of his designer suits. His flight from his house had been executed in a moment's panic as he realised how fast the police investigation was gaining ground.

He'd wanted to wait, wanted to taunt Detective

Hunter and her colleagues a little longer, but Oliver Tavender had insisted.

The safe receipt of the shipment was more important, after all.

The man was right, of course. A lot of money had already been invested, and he had four extremely powerful shareholders to answer to if the goods didn't arrive as scheduled.

Men whose reach extended well beyond the southern county's borders.

Men who could end his life at any given moment.

Oliver Tavender had worked tirelessly over the past three days to ensure all traces of his boss's life had been erased, and Demiri reluctantly admitted to himself that the man wasn't expendable.

It troubled him, to have to depend on one person so much, but he didn't have a choice. Not if he was to survive.

He knew when the time came that he would sacrifice Tavender to ensure his own freedom, and it troubled him that the man probably realised it.

He had no-one he could trust, and it was all Detective Hunter's fault.

He clenched his fist, resisting the urge to leave the safety of the building and hunt her down.

She would come to him, he knew it.

She wouldn't be able to resist.

He dropped his gaze to the road outside at movement to his right, but it was only the small silver hatchback that belonged to an old woman who lived half a mile away. He checked his watch, noted that her departure fitted the exact timing that had been observed every week for the past three months, and let his shoulders relax.

He turned from the window and moved over to a moth-eaten armchair, sinking into the soft cushions before reaching out to a small side table and picking up the large mug of soup that had been delivered to him minutes before by his host.

Tavender was away, running a final late afternoon errand that would erase a final piece of the puzzle for Detective Hunter and ensure Demiri could leave behind his legacy and start afresh.

He ran his eyes over the new passport that lay on the table, its rich burgundy colour embossed with the symbols of the European Union. He consoled himself with the fact he could still escape with ease and travel anywhere on the Continent, and had spent the past three days contemplating where best to set up his new operations.

It would take time, and money, but he had both.

It was the effect that running would have on his closely guarded reputation that worried him.

He had spent years growing the business, expanding it beyond the risky drugs empire he had first coveted and then discovering a whole new demand amongst his more elite customers.

He didn't count them as his equal, though. And they would be insulted if they thought he did.

To them, he was a supplier, nothing more.

He put down the mug of soup, steam rising from it on the cold air in the room, and picked up his notebook, tracing his thumb over the brown leather cover before slipping the band from around the pages and opening it to a page of neat handwriting.

Despite the assurances he'd always given to his clients, he kept a tally of their names, visits, and the money that passed between them. Together with the film that was kept on a server buried within the darkest reaches of the worldwide web, Demiri hoped he had enough insurance to keep them from hunting him for a while.

His thoughts returned to DS Hunter, and a pleasant shiver crossed his spine.

He'd heard, of course, that she hadn't been seen at either of his properties that morning, and for a moment he'd felt disappointment. It had soon been tempered with the realisation that perhaps her superiors thought her too valuable to be wasted on what turned out to be a fruitless search, and he settled back into the armchair, content in the knowledge that neither she nor his colleagues knew where he was, or of his plans for her.

His instructions to Tavender had been clear.

DS Hunter was his, and his alone.

He let the hot soup scald his mouth and throat, savouring the pain it brought, and stared at the bleak landscape beyond the window.

He would have his time with Detective Hunter, and soon.

# CHAPTER THIRTY-EIGHT

By the time the team returned to the incident room, a grey gloom had enveloped the town and a coolness had ended the afternoon, threatening rain.

A downcast Barnes had sunk into his chair before putting his feet up on the desk and resting his chin in his hand.

Kay placed a steaming mug of tea in front of him, and then frowned.

'Debbie? Have you seen DCI Harrison? I thought he wanted us all here for a briefing at half four?'

'Not for the past thirty minutes, no. Disappeared with his phone glued to his ear.'

Kay swallowed.

No doubt the DCI would be receiving the Chief Superintendent's thoughts on Demiri's disappearance, and in turn the team could expect short shrift when he returned.

Barnes scrunched up a note that had been stuck to

his computer screen by one of the administrative team members and lobbed it at the wastepaper basket, his top lip curling when it bounced off the side and fell to the floor instead.

They both looked up as Gavin opened the door, holding it open for Carys before the pair of them trudged towards their desks, their expressions downcast.

Sharp peered out from his office. 'Piper, Miles – grab yourselves a hot drink and we'll debrief.'

'D'you want to wait for Harrison, guv?' said Kay.

'No, I do not want to wait for bloody Harrison. It was his idea to have this debrief, so he can bloody well turn up on time. We'll start without him. Miles looks dead on her feet as it is.'

Carys gave him a wan smile and made her way over to the kettle.

Kay and Barnes wandered over to the whiteboard, quickly joined by the others.

Ten hours had already passed since the early morning briefing, and Kay was grateful Sharp had sent the junior members of the team home some time ago.

They would need their wits about them when they returned early the next day to begin sifting through the meagre information being processed by the forensic teams at Demiri's house and office in the hope of a breakthrough.

'Okay, Barnes. Give us a quick update on the search at Demiri's house,' said Sharp.

'There were no vehicles on the driveway when we arrived, guv. There's a separate building to the right of the house – an old stable block that had been converted into garages, with room for two vehicles – but that was empty.'

Barnes pointed with his mug of tea at the aerial image Sharp had set up on the whiteboard once more.

'The woodland around the property doesn't actually belong to Demiri – it's leased to him by the neighbouring farmer. Needless to say, there's an additional forensic team on site now, using GPS to check for any disturbed earth or other recent anomalies.'

'Was the house unlocked like the offices were?' said Gavin.

'No – we had to break down the front door. All the furniture was still there, but all of Demiri's personal effects are gone – clothing and the like – and there's no sign of any electronic equipment. Even the television's gone.'

'Cleared out in a hurry,' said Carys.

'No, and that's the thing,' said Barnes. 'I didn't get the sense that this was done in a panic. It felt too coordinated.'

'As if he was expecting us?' said Kay.

'Exactly.'

'When we interviewed him, he mentioned a new business venture in Romford,' said Sharp. 'Anything turn up about that?'

'No,' said Kay. 'I heard back from my contact at the Joint Intelligence Unit earlier, and they've come up empty-handed. I don't think Demiri has any business interests there. He was lying to us.'

'Well, at the moment he's done a disappearing act as famous as one of Pluckley's bloody ghosts,' said Barnes, then turned as Simon Harrison burst through the door and hurried towards them.

'Good, you're still here,' he said, tucking his mobile phone into his jacket pocket.

'What's going on?' said Sharp.

'The Chief Superintendent's agreed to holding a press conference at headquarters to talk about the Demiri case. If we hurry, we can get it on the six o'clock local news. National coverage will go out at nine o'clock tonight.'

'What?' Kay felt her jaw drop open, a moment too late. 'Sorry, guv. It's just that – do we want to tip him off about the investigation?'

Harrison's eyes darkened. 'Given the disaster of today's searches, I wouldn't say we've got a lot of choice, would you, Hunter? I mean, for goodness' sake – didn't either of you suspect *anything* when you interviewed him at his offices?'

'We didn't request the guided tour when we were there,' said Sharp through clenched teeth.

Harrison straightened his tie, and then glanced over his shoulder before beckoning them back towards the door.

'Well, it's too late now,' he said. 'Come on. We need to go. Demiri knows we're closing in on him. Right now, we've got him on the run. His business has closed, his offices are shut, and there's no sign of him at his house. He's hiding somewhere, and you know as well as

I do that if we do a televised appeal for information, someone close to him may come forward.'

Kay caught Sharp's glance in her direction, and shrugged before grabbing her jacket off the back of her chair and following him.

Based on her own involvement with Jozef Demiri, she doubted very much whether anyone who knew him would be brave – or stupid – enough to volunteer his whereabouts, despite Harrison's assertions.

From the expression Sharp wore, it was evident he thought the same, although he remained silent.

'Shall we take your car?' Harrison pushed through the door and strolled across the car park ahead of them.

'What's going on?' said Kay under her breath.

'No idea,' said Sharp. 'Keep your eyes open and your mouth shut. We'll reconvene after the press conference. Somewhere out of earshot from Mr Harrison and his sidekick, O'Reilly.'

'Right.'

# CHAPTER THIRTY-NINE

When they reached headquarters, various news vans and cars emblazoned with television channels' logos were jostling for space in the visitor car park.

Harrison checked his watch as he climbed from the passenger seat and waited while Sharp locked the car.

'We're running late,' he said, and hurried towards the building.

Kay cast her eyes over a nearby news vehicle as a technician slammed the door shut and looped a row of cable over his shoulder, whistling as he worked.

She scowled.

She knew news conferences were necessary to engage the public and seek information about ongoing investigations, but she despised the fact that it was often viewed as entertainment, a way to increase the evening's ratings, and that competition between the television channels would be high.

She glanced across at Sharp as they followed

Harrison, and noticed that he wore a similarly troubled expression.

They remained silent as they followed the detective chief inspector through the building and to the room that had been set aside for the news conference.

Kay stood on the threshold, and gathered her thoughts while she watched the various reporters, cameramen and photographers take their places.

A long table had been set up at one end of the room, a blue cloth covering its surface and a row of microphones taking up most of the space.

Various logos of familiar news channels were fastened to the microphones, each television station ensuring it received free advertising from its competitors' cameras.

Four chairs were behind the table, a glass of water in front of each.

A large panel emblazoned with the Kent Police logo had been erected behind the table, the Crime Stoppers telephone number clearly visible from the back of the room.

Despite the five rows of chairs that had been manhandled into the small room, reporters had to jostle for space around the edges, murmured reproaches from the camera operators reaching Kay's ears as she followed Harrison to the front of the room.

He gestured to the two seats to the right of the table. 'Sharp, if you take the one on the far right, with Hunter to your left. I'll be to her left, and then the Chief Superintendent will be to my left.' He lowered his voice. 'She's running a bit late, but hopefully she'll be here in the next couple of minutes. Some sort of last minute paperwork needs signing off on another investigation. I'll introduce everyone and read from the statement our media team has prepared. I'll defer to you if needs be.'

Kay moved between the table and the backdrop, gave Sharp a small smile as he pulled out her chair for her, and sat down. Reaching for her glass of water, she realised her hand was shaking and snatched it back. If Demiri was watching her from somewhere, she didn't want him to see her look anything but under control.

She had to let him know she was more than capable of bringing him to justice.

A sound at the back of the room to her left roused her from her thoughts, and she began to stand as the Chief Superintendent entered the room from a second doorway.

The woman waved her back into her seat. 'As you were, Hunter. How are we doing for time, Harrison?'

'We're still on schedule, ma'am. I arranged a bit of contingency knowing how busy you are.'

Kay turned her head and caught Sharp's amused eyes.

He winked, then took a sip from his water glass before leaning back in his chair, his hands clasped on the table in front of him.

Kay wished she felt as relaxed as he looked, then swivelled round to face the room once more as Harrison cleared his throat.

'Ladies and gentlemen, if you could take your seats, we'll make a start.'

He waited while the last of the reporters shuffled closer to the front of the room, microphones and phones held aloft, and then began.

Kay's eyes roamed the reporters' faces while he read from the prepared media statement, giving out the facts as known, and which had been deemed necessary to try and drive the investigation forward without giving Demiri too much information, before she was jolted from her observations by the sound of her name.

'I'd like to introduce the two lead detectives in this matter, Detective Inspector Sharp and Detective Sergeant Kay Hunter,' said Harrison. He swivelled in his seat to face Kay. 'Perhaps Detective Hunter would like to say something?'

Kay swallowed, then faced the crowded room and tried not to blink as a camera flash went off towards the back of it.

She'd been surprised at Harrison's insistence on her attending the press conference in the first place. She certainly hadn't imagined he'd introduce her by name and ask her to speak to the media.

She cleared her throat.

'We're very keen to speak to anyone who may have information that will assist with our enquiries,' she said. 'We believe Jozef Demiri is still in the area.'

She glanced to her right at Sharp and was rewarded with an almost imperceptible nod before he turned his attention to the reporters.

'Under no circumstances should Jozef Demiri be approached by the public,' he said. 'We consider him to be a danger, and possibly armed. Anyone who has information regarding his whereabouts is asked to please contact the incident room at Maidstone Police Station or through the Crime Stoppers number. I'll remind viewers that phone calls to the Crime Stoppers number are treated anonymously.'

He gestured to Harrison to wrap up the briefing, and Kay held her breath while the two senior detectives fielded questions from the journalists before Harrison leaned closer to the row of microphones.

'Ladies and gentlemen, thank you for your time. We'll let you know as soon as we have further details available for you.'

The Chief Superintendent rose from her seat, and led the way out the back door from the room.

She waited until Sharp closed it behind them before she spoke.

'Well done, Harrison. You'll keep me posted on developments?'

'We will, ma'am. Rest assured, if we receive any information as to the whereabouts of Demiri or his operations, we'll let you know immediately.'

'Thank you.'

She shook hands with all of them, and then strode away, extracting her mobile phone from the pocket of her uniform and placing it to her ear as she disappeared around a corner.

Harrison beamed as he watched her go, and then turned to Sharp and Kay.

'Good work, Hunter. Got the point across succinctly and clearly. No doubt we'll have more phone calls to work through by the morning.'

'Er, thanks, guv. Appreciated.'

Harrison glanced down as his mobile phone beeped. 'Right, well if you'll both excuse me, the Chief Super wants a quick word. I'll see you both tomorrow at oh seven hundred shall I, Sharp?'

'Will do,' said Sharp. He turned to Kay as the other detective strode away and turned a corner. 'Come on. I'll give you a lift back to the station, and then we'll take the team out for a drink and watch the press conference in the pub. Well done out there, by the way. At this rate, Harrison will be lining you up for interviews on daytime television.'

She began to follow him, then glanced up at his face, but his features remained impassive.

'You're joking, right?'

His mouth quirked, and she stopped dead in her tracks as he wandered off, whistling.

'Bastard,' she muttered.

# CHAPTER FORTY

Gavin swerved through the crowd holding a tray of drinks aloft before he reached the table at the back, and placed it in front of the team.

As one, they launched themselves at the pints of beer and clinked their glasses together.

'Well, let's hope it was worth it. With any luck, we'll have some new leads to work on in the morning,' said Barnes.

Sharp held his hand up to silence him, and then pointed at the television above the bar. 'It's on.'

Kay sipped her drink and watched over Carys's head as the news channel began to show the press conference.

Relief shot through her as she realised her nerves didn't show at all, and she was pleased that her voice sounded steady and authoritative.

Sharp swivelled round in his seat and held up his glass to hers.

'Good work.'

'Thanks.'

She fell silent as the news ended and the landlord turned down the volume, and let the sounds of the pub wash over her.

In the far corner, a group of three office workers stood around a quiz machine, their loud cheers interspersed with good-natured teasing, while next to them two men played a game of pool, the familiar sound of wood on resin carrying across to where she sat.

She felt her shoulders relax as she listened to the good-natured banter between her colleagues.

'So,' said Carys. 'Are we talking off the record while we're here?'

'Cone of silence,' said Barnes, and took a gulp of beer.

'We can.' Sharp swept imaginary dust from the table, and then rested his elbows on it. 'What did you want to know?'

'Did Harrison use that press conference to further the investigation, or his own career?'

Gavin sucked in his breath, before slapping Carys on the back. 'It was nice working with you, Miles.'

'She's got a point,' said Kay. 'It does make you wonder what he was trying to achieve. He could have released a normal press release instead of holding a press conference. As it was, he didn't allow a lot of time for questions.'

'In all fairness, he was probably trying to ensure that

the journalists had all the details in time to make the six o'clock news,' said Sharp, and jerked his thumb over his shoulder to the now silent television. 'And, there are more people that watch TV than read newspapers these days. I would imagine our media team will be uploading that to all our social media as we speak. So, I think he used it to further the investigation.'

Kay glanced across at Carys, and noticed the younger detective looked chastened.

'However,' said Sharp, the corner of his mouth twitching, 'I'm sure it didn't do his career any harm.'

They burst out laughing, and then fell into companionable silence once more.

'I wonder what the Chief Super wanted to speak to him about afterwards?' said Kay eventually.

Sharp shrugged. 'It's all politics over there. I'm sure Harrison's going to use this case to his advantage somehow.'

'You don't mind? Him coming in and taking the lead?'

He shook his head. 'I want to put Demiri away. That's all that matters.' He grimaced. 'I'm not sure I'd want to be in Harrison's shoes, anyway.'

'Enough shop talk!' said Barnes, and stood. 'Next round's on me. Same again?'

————

Two hours and a curry later, Kay leaned forward and tapped the taxi driver on the shoulder.

'It's the one on the right, just past the shop.'

'Right you are.'

The vehicle slowed as it rounded the bend, in time for Kay to see a car pulling away from outside her house at speed.

Its brake lights flared at the end of the road, before it turned right and out of sight.

Her heart slammed against her ribs.

The taxi driver braked, and switched on the interior light.

'That's ten pounds fifty, love.'

'Thanks.'

She paid the taxi driver and hurried towards her front door, her breath fogging in the cold autumn night.

As she approached the front door, the security lights flickered on, and she paced back and forth across the gravel, her eyes sweeping across the stony surface for any trace of who had been there.

Large footprints had sunk into the gravel, but she couldn't work out if they belonged to Adam or her mysterious visitor.

She made her way back to the front door, and as she inserted her key into the lock, the two guinea pigs began their high-pitched squeaking.

She cursed under her breath, realising that they were probably starving after not being fed for nearly twelve hours, and stumbled into the hallway.

The sole of her foot slid across the doormat, and she glanced down and frowned, before picking up the business card that lay face down on the rough surface.

A short note had been scrawled across the plain white back of the card.

*Call me, please. We need to talk.*

She flipped it over, and swore again.

*Jonathan Aspley, Kentish Times.*

'Bloody Harrison.'

Satisfied her night-time visitor posed no threat to her safety, only her temper, and cursing the DCI once more for his insistence on her presence at the press conference, she slammed the front door shut, slid the bolts across and stomped towards the kitchen, flicking on light switches as she went.

She dumped her handbag on the worktop and picked up the plastic box containing the guinea pig food, crouching down to their hutch.

'Hey, you two. Sorry I'm late.'

Clyde made an irritated sound in his throat, then buried his face in the fresh food. Bonnie's bright reproachful eyes stared up at Kay, before she too bustled over to the food bowl.

Kay refilled their water bottle, and then straightened and tucked her hair behind her ears before grabbing a glass and filling it from the kitchen tap.

She'd had two pints of beer at the pub before switching to sparkling water at the Indian restaurant, but she knew the spicy food would leave her thirsty. After the early start, she wanted a decent night's sleep.

She padded over to the worktop and pulled out one of the bar stools before sinking onto it with a sigh.

As if on cue, her mobile phone began to ring.

She groaned, and reached out for her bag, a smile forming as she recognised Adam's number.

'I thought you were at work,' she said by way of answering.

'Late one?'

'Not too bad. We went out for a curry afterwards.'

'I'm jealous. The hotel food is terrible.'

'How did your trip to the stables go?'

'Fantastic, but bloody cold. He's got some great ideas, and I think we'll be able to work together.'

'That's great.'

'It is, isn't it? Listen – I'll have to make it quick, because we're in the middle of dinner and I've just nipped out to call you. My flight back might be delayed. Apparently, there's a bad weather front heading this way, and we might get fogged in.'

Kay swallowed, but hid her disappointment from her voice.

'That's a pain. Do they know how long for?'

'A day or so, maybe. I'll let you know as soon as I can.'

'Okay.'

'I've got to go. Love you.'

'Love you too.'

Kay ended the call, then pushed the phone across the worktop and made her way out to the panel next to the front door.

In her haste to feed the guinea pigs, she'd forgotten to set the security alarm.

It might've only been a journalist at her door earlier

that evening, but she wasn't prepared to take her chances.

Not now that Demiri would know she was an active part of the investigation to bring him to justice once and for all.

# CHAPTER FORTY-ONE

Kay was grateful the incident room was quiet when she arrived at work the next morning.

Despite her plans to get a decent night's sleep, she'd spent the early hours tossing and turning, rehearsing in her mind what she was going to say to Harrison about the reporter finding out where she lived.

Barnes and Piper were nowhere to be seen, and Carys had her phone to her ear as Kay dumped her bag under her desk and stalked towards Sharp's office door.

She rapped her knuckles against it twice, and fought down her anger.

It wouldn't do to take out her frustration on her senior officer, but she did want to make it clear that her personal life was off limits.

'Come in.'

Sharp's voice resonated through the wooden surface, and she twisted the handle.

To her surprise, DCI Harrison was already present, twisting in one of the visitor chairs to face her.

'Morning, Hunter.'

'Good morning. Can I have a word, please?'

'Of course,' said Sharp, and waved her to the spare seat.

Kay noted Harrison had learned his lesson and had taken the more comfortable one.

He was a fast learner, she had to give him credit for that.

'What seems to be the problem?'

'This.'

She held up the journalist's card. 'When I got home last night, this man's car was leaving my driveway. He left this card behind. I'd like to know how he found out where I live.'

'What's his name?' said Sharp.

'Jonathan Aspley.'

A sneer curled Harrison's top lip.

'The man's a pain in the backside,' he said. 'I'd advise you don't contact him. I'll tell the media team to get in touch with him and answer any questions he's got. I need my officers working this case, not dealing with reporters.'

'Kay's got a point though,' said Sharp. 'We need to ascertain how he found out where she lives. I don't mind my officers helping out with a press conference to raise awareness of our investigation, but I draw the line at them being contacted directly.'

Harrison leaned forward and clicked his fingers, and

when Kay didn't react he plucked the card from her grasp and glanced at the note on the back. 'Ignore him. If he contacts you again, let me know and I'll have words.'

Kay could sense the dismissal in his voice, and decided not to push her luck.

'Thanks, guv.'

She left Sharp's office, closing the door behind her and crossed the incident room to her desk.

Leafing through a pile of paperwork that had been left in her tray, she tucked her desk phone between her ear and shoulder and began to work through the voicemail messages that had been left.

Two were from the DS she'd passed on her existing caseload to, and by the time she'd phoned him back and they'd chatted about two of the burglary cases he was managing on her behalf, it was mid-morning.

A loud voice from the corridor preceded Barnes entering the incident room, closely followed by Gavin whose face was grey.

Kay bit her lip. The young detective constable had been handpicked by Sharp to attend the post mortem of the three victims discovered at the smallholding with Barnes, and it had clearly taken its toll.

'What's Lucas's preliminary findings?' she said as Barnes dropped into the seat at his desk.

'Asphyxiation of two of them, and a broken neck for the third, as we suspected,' he said, his voice weary.

Kay pushed away her paperwork and leaned back with a sigh.

'He also reckons they were beaten before being killed,' said Barnes. 'The oldest victim – the one that's been there the longest I mean – had a broken shin bone and wrist. The other two had broken fingers. There's evidence of them being raped multiple times, too.'

Kay ran a hand through her hair, and tried not to picture the women's last moments.

'Jesus, Barnes.'

'Yeah. I know.'

Her eyes flickered across the room to where Gavin sat, his chin in his hand as he scrolled through emails.

'He's taken it badly.'

'He has an older sister the same age as the latest victim.'

Kay nodded. 'Any luck tracing their identities?'

Barnes shook his head. 'No. I've got a horrible feeling we're not going to find any, either.' He sighed, and leaned forward. 'Anyway, what's been happening here this morning? What juicy gossip have I missed?'

Carys and Gavin wandered over, coffee mugs in hand, their faces inquisitive at Barnes's question.

'What was that all about, earlier?' Carys said, jerking her head towards the closed door of Sharp's office.

Kay lowered her voice and told them about the journalist that had left his card at her house the previous night, and Harrison's assertions that he'd get the media department to inform the reporter that turning up at detectives' homes wouldn't be tolerated.

'It's all Harrison's fault. I never wanted to be on the news,' she grumbled.

'Not so long ago, you'd have killed for an opportunity like this,' said Barnes.

'Not so long ago, I was happily working under the radar,' she fumed.

Barnes fanned his face theatrically. 'Oh, I'm a celebrity! I can't handle the pressure!'

Kay crossed her arms over her chest and glared at him while Carys and Gavin dissolved into laughter.

'Sometimes, Ian Barnes, you're a right pain in the—'

'Looks like everyone's having fun here. What's going on?'

Kay swivelled her chair round to see O'Reilly strolling towards them rubbing his hands together, a broad grin across his face.

She smiled. 'Oh, nothing. Too hard to explain.'

'Well, it's good to know you can all keep your sense of humour in the circumstances. That's the way,' he added, slapping Gavin on the back as he moved towards his own desk.

Gavin glared at him until Carys gave him a nudge.

'Be nice,' she hissed.

'I don't need to be,' he said. 'You're being nice enough for all of us.'

He turned on his heel and stormed towards the whiteboard where he stood, glaring at it while he finished the rest of his coffee.

Crestfallen, Carys turned to Kay, but she shook her head.

'You're on your own with that one.'

'Hey, look at this.'

Kay turned to see Debbie approaching, her notebook in her hand.

'What've you got?'

'A bloke phoned the hotline. Says he saw the press conference and reckons he saw something on the beach below his house two nights ago.'

'Got a name?'

'Adrian Webster. Lives in a village called Amesworth – it's about six miles from Dymchurch.'

'They've had issues with illegal entrants landing at Dymchurch before, Sarge,' said Gavin. 'Could be worth a look.'

'I reckon,' said Kay. 'Got a phone number for him?'

'Yes. And an address,' said Debbie.

'What's going on?'

Kay glanced over her shoulder at the interruption to see Harrison striding towards her, Sharp in his wake.

'Might have a lead.' She indicated to Debbie to update the two senior officers.

'That's a great start,' said Harrison. 'Right, I want you all down there now. Interview as many of the locals as you can, starting with those who have houses nearest the beach.'

'What about local uniform?'

'I'm sure we can rustle a few of them up to help with door-to-door enquiries.'

Kay glanced out the window at the grey skies and clouds being buffeted along by a chill wind, and groaned inwardly before turning back to the DCI.

Harrison was smiling.

'What did I tell you?' he said. 'The press conference worked.'

# CHAPTER FORTY-TWO

Kay shoved her hands deep into her coat pockets, grateful she'd remembered to put the thick wool garment on the back seat of the car before leaving the police station.

Beside her, Carys bundled a scarf around her neck, squinting against the bitter wind that whipped off the sea and around the exposed car park.

'I'm beginning to wish I'd brought one of those.'

'My dad always told me to wear a scarf and cover my wrists and ankles,' said Carys. 'It works. I haven't had a cold in years.'

Kay narrowed her eyes and peered across the car park as another vehicle slowed and turned onto the gravel, its chassis creaking as it bumped and swayed over the potholed surface.

Barnes climbed from the passenger seat as the car drew to a stop next to hers.

'I swear blind the suspension's gone on half the

bloody pool vehicles,' he grumbled, before being buffeted by a gust of wind. 'Flipping heck. Not exactly the Costa del Sol, is it?'

'I'm sure it's pleasant in the summer,' said Kay.

The older detective didn't look convinced.

'I can't imagine how desperate someone must be to try and cross that,' said Gavin as he joined them, pocketing the car keys.

They turned towards the water, the dark grey waves tumbling and boiling across the surface.

'Fancy a surf, Gav?' said Carys.

'No thanks – I'd have hypothermia in seconds.'

Kay flipped up the collar of her coat. 'Right, let's get on with it. Uniform have three patrols starting at the opposite end of the village, so with any luck we'll get this done by mid-afternoon and make it back in time for the briefing. We'll split up into pairs so, Carys – you're with me. We'll take one side of the street each.'

The others murmured their agreement.

'Last one to the café at the end buys the hot drinks,' said Barnes.

'Deal.'

'Which house do you want to start with?' said Carys as Barnes and Gavin walked away.

Kay pointed to a small weather-beaten cottage nearest to the car park. 'That's the house we've got the address for Adrian Webster, so we'll start with him. From there, we'll work our way back.'

They trudged across the mud-specked gravel to the cottage, and Kay noticed a wisp of smoke escape the brick chimney before being whisked away on the wind. As they drew closer, the building didn't appear as dilapidated as she'd first thought, and instead its walls were covered with a naked wisteria, its leaves shrivelled while it waited for spring to appear.

The door opened as Carys pushed through the low gate set into the wall, and an elderly man peered out, a china mug in his hand.

'You're Detective Hunter, right?'

'Yes,' said Kay, her brow furrowing.

'I recognise you from the telly,' he said, beaming. 'Adrian Webster.'

Kay fought down the urge to roll her eyes, took the outstretched hand, and introduced Carys.

'Lovely to meet you. Kettle's boiled. Come on in.'

They stamped their feet on the doormat to loosen the detritus that clung to their soles before he pointed to his right with his mug.

'Go on through. I'll bring a tray in.'

Kay led the way into a living room that showed its age, despite Webster's attempts at decoration.

'You live on your own?' said Carys when he returned with their drinks.

'Yes, my wife died three years ago.' He shrugged. 'Cancer. It was a blessing in the end, to be honest.'

'When you phoned our colleagues earlier, you mentioned you might have some information that could help us?' said Kay.

Webster laid his mug on a coaster on the table in front of them before easing back into his chair and placing his hands in his lap. 'Yes. I don't know if it's much, but I thought I'd better say something, you know? Especially as you went to so much effort with the press conference and everything. You look just like you do on telly, by the way.'

Kay nodded and took a sip of her tea, figuring he'd take the hint and keep talking.

'Well,' he said, 'since Sarah died I don't sleep that well anymore. I find myself lying there thinking about things too much, so about a year ago I got into the habit of getting up, putting on the electric fire down here and making a hot drink. I like to sit at the window and watch the sea. It's calming.'

He shrugged, as if to clear a memory that cut too deep. 'Anyway, there've been a couple of things lately that had me wondering. Lights on the water that seem to be heading this way, but then cut out before they get too close sometimes. I go for a walk during the night occasionally, to blow the cobwebs away. Always have, even when Sarah was alive, but about a week or so ago I was about to go back upstairs when the clouds parted, and I thought I saw a dinghy or something pull up to the shoreline.'

'Did you see anyone in it?'

'I saw someone run down to the boat – goodness knows where they'd been hiding, because you've seen the landscape here. Flat as a pancake. But I can't be sure I saw anyone get *out* of the boat – the moon disappeared behind clouds again, and I couldn't see anything else. I got a bit nosy, and it wasn't too cold back then, so I nipped out the front door to see if I could spot anyone else.'

'That could've been incredibly dangerous, Mr Webster,' said Kay.

He gave her a rueful smile. 'I only thought about that afterwards,' he said. 'I was too interested in what was happening. Anyway, I was too late to see whatever it is that was going on, because by the time I got to the gate I could hear the engine revving as the boat left the beach.'

'Why didn't you report it at the time?'

He shrugged. 'I have, in the past, but nothing ever happens. I gave up. You're the first ones to have taken me seriously.'

'Could you see anyone on the beach after the boat left?'

Webster shook his head. 'The place was deserted.'

'What about the next day? Was there anything lying around – any items that looked out of place?'

'No,' he said. 'It's like they were never there.'

# CHAPTER FORTY-THREE

After thanking Adrian Webster for his time and reluctantly leaving the warmth of his house, Kay followed Carys through the gate and out onto the coast road, then glanced over her shoulder as they began to walk away.

The net curtain at the living room window twitched, a silhouette moving beyond her line of sight before disappearing.

She pursed her lips.

'What're you thinking, Sarge?'

Kay gritted her teeth as a bitter wind caught her hair and assaulted her face and ears before she tugged up her jacket collar and burrowed her chin into the thick material. 'Well, we'll obviously have to see if the incident he mentioned ties in with anyone else's statement, but we'll run it past Sharp at the briefing later on. I can't believe he didn't report it at the time, though.'

'Well, like he said – he and other locals have reported it before, but it keeps happening.' Carys sighed. 'I don't envy Colin Fox and his lot. It must be so frustrating for them.'

'Yeah, I suppose. Do me a favour when we get back to the station, though. Go through HOLMES2 and find out if he really did report anything prior to this, or whether he's wasting our time.'

'Think your celebrity status went to his head?'

Kay narrowed her eyes as dimples appeared in Carys's cheeks.

'Very funny.'

Kay lifted her gaze to the road beyond, now a rough track that had narrowed to a single car width. Squinting against the wind, she spotted Barnes and Piper leaving a property at the far end.

Beyond them, in the distance, an imposing brick monolith rose from the flat landscape; a Victorian water tower that had been battered by the elements over the centuries and now stood sentient over the small hamlet that surrounded it.

Barnes lifted his hand before both men turned and disappeared from sight.

Kay ran her tongue over her lips, the tang of salt reminding her of childhood holidays on the Devon coastline. She glanced to her left as they made their way towards the next house, a scrubby patch of grass dividing the coast road and the beach beyond.

Somehow, the Kentish coastline had always seemed more desolate to her; alien. The flat marshes to the east of the county had never endeared themselves to her when she'd ventured there on walks with Adam when she'd first arrived in the area. Instead, the landscape set her nerves on edge as she'd peered through mist at abandoned fishing boats, whilst the southern fringes of the county left her with a feeling of melancholy every time she visited, even in the summer.

She blinked to clear the thought as the boundary to the next cottage began, and noticed that unlike the previous property they'd visited, the garden to the rear connected with the beach beyond.

The front of the house was framed with a low wall matching the style of that bordering the rest of the street, with a white iron gate leading to a front door.

She sniffed, the strong aroma of a cigarette wafting on the breeze as Carys rang the bell.

No sound came from inside the house, and Carys knocked twice before dropping her hand and turning to Kay.

'What do you think, Sarge?'

'Round the back.'

She led the way along the worn gravel path past the front window of the house and around the side of the building, her eyes taking in the ivy that clung to the walls and up alongside a single window near the pitched roof.

As she reached the back of the house, the wind whipped up a dust devil, blowing sand into her eyes.

'Shit,' she muttered, lowering her head and blinking to clear the grit.

'You okay?'

'Yes.'

She reached into her bag and tugged a paper handkerchief from a packet before blowing her nose and blinking once more.

Carys shielded her eyes with her hand and then pointed at a wooden hulled boat that hugged the tufts of grass poking through the sand. 'Over there.'

They moved closer, and Kay noticed a puff of smoke appear towards the bow before a head popped up above the level of the hull at the sound of their footsteps.

A man in his late sixties with a woollen beanie hat pulled low over his ears peered at them, a look of confusion across his face.

'What do you want?'

Kay held up her warrant card. 'DS Kay Hunter and DC Carys Miles of Kent Police. We were wondering if you could help us with some enquiries we're making in the area?'

He removed the cigarette from his mouth, blew smoke to one side, then narrowed his eyes before dropping a hammer into the boat.

'What about?'

'We understand from some of your neighbours that there's been some suspicious activity along the coastline here. We're trying to ascertain if the beach here is being used to land illegal entrants.'

Kay moved around the vessel to join him.

'You been talking to that Webster up the road? He's

always saying he sees things. Can't always take his word for granted.' He snorted, and gestured to the wide expanse of the beach stretching out behind where they stood. 'Mind you, smugglers always loved this coastline,' he said. 'Brandy, tea, tobacco – and now people. Hasn't changed for centuries.'

'Sorry – didn't catch your name?'

'Tom Harcourt.'

'How long have you lived here, Tom?'

'About fifteen years.'

'Do you have an interest in the history of the place?'

'I suppose so. I moved down here from Wiltshire after I got divorced.'

'Thought I recognised the accent. It's a long way from Wiltshire.'

He shrugged. 'The house belonged to a great-uncle of mine. He left it to me in his will. I needed to live somewhere different after losing Celia.'

Kay ran her gaze over the lines of the boat. 'Do you fish?'

'Only for myself. Not commercially. Sometimes it's just good to get out on the water, and away from the land. Gives me time to think.'

Kay wandered over to the barbed wire fence that separated the property from the beach and plucked at a small feather caught on one of the sharp spikes. 'This fence a recent addition?'

'Not much else I can do. Can't afford one of those fancy alarm systems.'

He brushed past her and headed towards the house,

then removed the cigarette stub from his mouth and dropped it into a bright blue children's beach bucket filled with sand next to the back door.

'Have you seen any suspicious activity recently?' said Carys.

He scratched his ear. 'No. But I hear bits and pieces. Webster did mention lights on the beach late at night.'

'And you didn't report it?'

'What's the point, love? Even if Webster's not imagining things, your lot and that Border Agency bunch can't do anything about it, can you? You stop one boat, there'll be three more ready to take its place on the next night's tide.' He sighed. 'It's all very well going on about how they're increasing security at the ferry terminals and Eurotunnel, but where does that leave us? I remember ten years ago round here, no-one locked their doors at night. Now we're having stuff stolen left, right and centre.'

Kay snapped her notebook closed, unable to provide the man with the answers he sought. She fished out a business card.

'My direct number's on there. Mobile, too. If you do see anything, or perhaps hear something over the next few days, you'll give me a call?'

'I suppose so.'

'Thanks.'

# CHAPTER FORTY-FOUR

Kay sank into her seat and glanced at her mobile phone to check for messages before dumping it on the desk.

The incident room held an atmosphere of despair. News had quickly spread that the four detectives and the team of uniformed officers who had travelled to Amesworth had not succeeded in getting the results that they'd hoped for.

Kay herself couldn't help thinking that it had been a total waste of time. She couldn't understand why Harrison had insisted on her travelling to speak with Adrian Webster, when the man had very little information to give them. In fact, it would have been better use of her time and that of the other detectives if an interview had been conducted by phone instead.

Sharp paced the floor in front of the whiteboard, his impatience with the slow progress of the investigation all too evident.

Carys moved between them, handing out coffee

she'd picked up from their favourite café on returning to the police station. 'I can't understand why someone would want to live somewhere quite so desolate,' she said, leaning on Kay's desk and sipping from her own hot drink. 'God, that's better. I couldn't feel the tips of my fingers for a while there.'

'You're not kidding,' said Kay. 'The heater's broken in the car Gavin was driving, too.'

She'd elected to swap places with Barnes on the way back, leaving the older detective to travel with Carys so she could catch up with Gavin and listen to his feedback about their door-to-door enquiries prior to the briefing.

She also took the time to ask how he was feeling after the triple post mortem he'd had to attend the previous day. Her instincts had been right; the young detective was struggling.

'I know I shouldn't get upset,' he said, steering the car round a series of bends on the tail of Carys and Barnes's vehicle. 'But I can't get the images out of my head. And the smell...'

'You're human, Gavin,' she'd said. 'And that's what's going to make you a great detective. Having said that, if you're struggling and need to speak to someone about it, don't leave it too late, okay? It can be done anonymously. No-one needs to know.'

A faint smile had crossed his face. 'Thanks, Sarge. I appreciate it.'

They'd said no more about the matter, and now Gavin sat poised and listening attentively as Sharp addressed the room.

'Did you learn anything useful from these people?' said the DI. 'I thought this Adrian Webster chap was the one who called the hotline after the press conference?'

'He was,' said Kay. 'He's a bit of an insomniac and reports seeing movement at night out on the beach, but couldn't give us any hard evidence to suggest what he'd seen was a boat landing, and he only reports seeing one person on the beach for a brief moment. Another resident of Amesworth we spoke to, Tom Harcourt, suggested that Webster was imagining things.'

Sharp chucked the pen he'd been holding on to the desk next to the whiteboard and ran a hand over his face. 'So, he could've been suffering from delusions caused by lack of sleep, then?'

Kay shrugged. She wasn't prepared to add fuel to his foul mood.

'Or he just wanted to meet Hunter after her television appearance,' said Barnes.

Kay glared at him, but conceded the point. It had happened before to other detectives; sometimes the public simply wanted to feel a part of an investigation because there was nothing else in their lives.

'Doesn't seem to be a close community,' said Gavin, leafing through the pages of his notebook. 'When we spoke to a Mrs Greaves at the Dymchurch end of the village, she had no idea who lived two doors up from her, even though she'd lived there for nearly eight years and they were there when she arrived.'

'It's because the place doesn't have a pub,' said Barnes.

'What's that got to do with it?' said Debbie.

'Like Gavin said, there's no sense of community. If there was a pub, people would have somewhere to congregate. Instead, they keep to themselves.'

'Doesn't have a church, either.'

'The pub would have a bigger audience.'

'It's a fair point,' said Kay, catching sight of Sharp's look of exasperation and deciding to steer the conversation back to the investigation. 'None of them have a reason to socialise with each other, and they all seem suspicious of what each other is up to – or they don't care.'

Sharp's response was interrupted by Kay's desk phone ringing, and he indicated to her to take the call while he finalised the briefing.

Hopeful that a new lead had eventuated from the press conference or from their conversations with local residents that day, she raced to answer it before the caller changed their mind.

'Hello? DS Hunter speaking.'

'Detective Hunter – it's Jonathan Aspley from the *Kentish*—'

'I've got no time to speak to a reporter. We're in the middle of a—'

'Please. It's not about your investigation. Well, not directly.' Aspley exhaled, and seemed to gather his thoughts before continuing. 'Don't let on to your colleagues you're speaking with me, okay? I need to meet you so we can talk in private.'

Kay turned away from the rest of the team, who

were now starting to wander back to their desks, the briefing concluded, and lowered her voice.

'I'm not giving you an exclusive, Aspley. What the hell do you take me for?'

'This isn't about you helping me,' he said. 'It's about me helping you. Can we meet? I promise, I won't waste your time. It's important.'

Kay checked her watch. 'Okay. Where?'

# CHAPTER FORTY-FIVE

After making an excuse that she had to pick up some information from Grey's digital forensics team at HQ, Kay left the incident room and hurried down to the reception desk.

Sergeant Hughes looked up from his newspaper, and raised an eyebrow.

'In a rush?'

'Can I have a pool car, please Hughes?'

He sucked in his breath. 'Well, I'm not sure—'

'*Please*. Sorry – haven't got time to mess around.'

He pushed the paper aside and wiggled the mouse until his computer screen lit up. 'Where's your car?'

'Parked outside the White Rabbit. We went for drinks after work last night.'

'Revelling in your newfound celebrity status?'

'Don't you start.'

He smirked, jabbed at the keyboard with two

fingers, and then reached into a drawer and handed her a set of keys. 'It's yours for two hours.'

'Thanks.'

She bolted from the reception area and along the corridor that led to the car park, thanking two uniformed officers under her breath as they stood to one side as she ran past, bemused expressions on their faces.

She checked her watch again before turning the key in the ignition of the small hatchback Hughes had assigned to her.

Aspley had told her he'd wait twenty minutes. After that, he'd take her nonappearance as a sign she wasn't interested in what he had to say.

His chosen location, Mote Park, was a popular open space in the centre of the town covering over four hundred and fifty acres. With a mixture of grassland, wooded areas, rivers and a large lake, it had been in existence since Mediaeval times.

Kay shook her head slightly to clear the image of a hanged man that had been discovered in the park a year ago.

Instead, her thoughts turned to what the journalist wanted to speak to her about. His insistence that it wasn't to do with the press conference piqued her interest.

She pulled into the car park ten minutes later, and hurried from the vehicle towards a figure standing next to the deserted picnic tables.

'Jonathan Aspley?'

He held out his hand. 'Detective Hunter. Thanks for agreeing to meet with me.'

'I don't appreciate reporters turning up at my house uninvited.'

'I'm sorry. I needed to talk to you away from the police station.'

Kay frowned. 'Why?'

His eyes shifted from her to the car park, and then he glanced over his shoulder. 'Do you mind if we walk?'

She narrowed her eyes. 'Are you wearing a wire?'

'No!' He flicked open his jacket. 'No, I'm not. You can check if you want.'

Kay shook her head, fought down her frustration at his cloak and dagger attitude, and gestured to him to lead the way.

She let him walk a little ahead of her, to give her time to study him.

She hadn't had a chance to look him up on a newspaper website, and he was younger than he had sounded on the phone.

A little shorter than she was, he wore his light brown hair longer at the front and she noticed he had a habit of flicking it out of his eyes before speaking. His pale blue eyes gave his already cool features a washed-out look, especially in the weak winter light.

She turned her attention to her surroundings as she trudged after him.

Where in the summer an ice-cream van would be stationary, surrounded by harassed parents and fractious children, the area now stood empty, a smattering of wizened leaves chasing across the broken and pock-marked asphalt.

Gnarled tree roots broke the edges of the path, naked limbs above creaking in the wind.

Aspley waited until they had drawn level with the boathouse before he slowed down, his gaze drawn to a pair of swans on the lake to the right.

Kay hugged her coat to her chest and squinted against the sharp breeze that lifted her hair from her collar.

'If you need to tell me something, could you hurry up? It's bloody freezing out here.'

'Sorry. I wanted us to talk somewhere where I could be sure we wouldn't be overheard.'

'What's going on?'

'How well do you know Simon Harrison?'

She shrugged. 'This is the first time I've worked with him. He's from SOCU, so I haven't had anything to do with him before. Why?'

Aspley blew his cheeks out before responding.

'I've been investigating Harrison's method of policing for a while now. When I realised he'd relocated to Kent from the Met three years ago, I applied for a position on the newspaper here so I could follow him.'

Kay gestured to a wooden bench at the lake's edge. 'All right. You've got my attention.'

They moved across to the seat, and Aspley buttoned up his jacket before continuing.

'While he was in the Met, Harrison gained a

reputation for doing anything to further his career. He put a lot of criminals away, but there's always been a question mark over his methods.'

'What do you mean?'

'Before he was transferred out, a detective working with him was murdered by a suspect they'd been pursuing for six months.'

Kay swallowed. 'That must have been terrible for him, to have that on his conscience.'

'Harrison doesn't have a conscience. He used his colleague to set up the suspect, and it went wrong. Sound familiar?'

Kay's thoughts turned to Gareth Jenkins, and a sickness began in her stomach. 'If Harrison was responsible for his colleague's death, there would've been a Professional Standards investigation, and he would have been relieved from duty.'

'He made a deal. He took the transfer, and the file was closed.'

'What's this all got to do with me?'

'That's my point, Kay. He's using you to bait Demiri. Why else would he ask you to turn up at the press conference?'

Kay snorted. 'Don't be ridiculous. It was my idea to be part of his team.'

'Was it? Or did he simply give you the impression it was your idea?'

She narrowed her eyes at him, then thought of all the times Harrison had disappeared without a trace during the short time she'd been working with him, and wondered how desperate he was to ensure she and the rest of Sharp's team would be kept at arm's length from being the ones to arrest Demiri.

Would he go as far as bribing a journalist to try to frighten her off? Try to make her doubt her own assertions that he'd made her an integral part of his investigation, only to seize any chance he could to undermine her capabilities?

Or, was the journalist attempting to cause paranoia, in the hope that she'd confide in him?

She rose from the bench and glared at Aspley. 'This conversation is over.'

Kay shoved her hands in her pockets and spun on her heel.

'Wait!'

She stopped, and glanced over her shoulder. 'What?'

Aspley stood next to the bench, his expression pained. 'Look, be careful, all right?'

She pursed her lips, and shook her head. 'Nice try, Aspley. Now, if you'll excuse me, I've got an investigation to get on with.'

She turned and hurried towards the car, not trusting herself to look back again, and her mind working overtime.

# CHAPTER FORTY-SIX

Kay sat bolt upright in bed, her heart pounding, her thoughts confused as she was pulled from a deep sleep.

'What the—'

A series of loud squeaks hit a crescendo from the kitchen below, and she reached out blindly for the bedside lamp, shielding her eyes as the lightbulb winked to life.

She held her wrist closer to her face and squinted as she tried to read her watch dial, a moment before her mobile phone began to ring and vibrate across the surface of the dressing table.

She groaned and flipped back the duvet, stumbling across the room to pick up the phone before it went to voicemail.

The alarm hadn't been due to go off for another ten minutes, and yet here she was with two fur-balls yelling for their breakfast, and no doubt a crisis at work.

'Hello?' she mumbled.

'It's Sharp.'

'What's up?'

'Reg Powers at the garage near Hythe has been found dead. How long until you can get here?'

Kay did a quick calculation in her head. 'About an hour and a half?'

'Make it quicker if you can. Bring Barnes.'

He ended the call without waiting for an answer, and Kay cursed under her breath before hitting the speed dial for Barnes.

'Ughhh.'

'Morning.'

'What time is it?'

'Quarter to six. Reg Powers has been found dead. Sharp wants us to attend the scene. Can you pick me up as soon as possible?'

'Okay.'

She flicked through the screen on her phone until she found the alarm, switched it off and tossed the phone onto the bed before making her way through to the en suite. Pulling her t-shirt over her head, she stepped under the warm jets of water and wiped the sleep from her eyes as she processed Sharp's news.

Hurrying downstairs, she threw food into the guinea pigs' bowl and then swiped her bag off the worktop.

Unlocking the door, she hurried to the end of the driveway to wait for Barnes.

It was already feeling like it was going to be a long day.

———

Kay unbuckled her seatbelt as Barnes braked alongside the kerb several metres from the garage, and leapt from the car before he'd switched off the engine.

Her eyes swept over the scene as she approached, and her heart sank.

A television news van was parked opposite the garage forecourt, which had been sectioned off by strips of crime scene tape fluttering in the bitter morning air.

A reporter was risking life and limb by standing in the middle of the road, speaking to the camera trained on her and gesturing excitedly to the white tents that had been set up to act as a screen between the street and the garage.

Her bright red suit hurt Kay's non-caffeinated eyes.

Kay wandered over and waited until the woman had finished her spiel and lowered her microphone.

'Perfect, Suzie,' called the cameraman.

'Excuse me,' said Kay.

The woman raised an eyebrow that had been plucked within an inch of its life. 'Yes?'

Kay raised her warrant card, and then pointed to the blind corner in the road behind the woman. 'This is a main thoroughfare, and has a sixty mile speed limit. To save my colleagues from Traffic having to scrape up what's left of you when the next heavy goods vehicle comes along, would you mind conducting your interviews on the pavement?'

The woman stuck out her bottom lip. 'It won't have the same effect. Joe won't be able to get the right angle.'

'Well, Joe's going to have a bloody fantastic shot of you getting splattered across the road if you don't do as I say.'

The reporter sighed, flicked her jet black hair over her shoulder and flounced away, grumbling loudly to the cameraman.

'Making friends and influencing people, Sarge?'

'Honestly, Barnes. You'd think they'd have some common sense.'

They turned their attention back to the garage, crossing the road and signing a clipboard that a uniformed officer held out to them.

He noted their names, and then lifted the tape.

'DI Sharp's over there, with the CSI team leader,' he said.

'Cheers,' said Kay. She paused, and let Barnes walk on ahead of her. 'Any issues with the reporter?'

He grinned. 'No – she's staying well away. More's the pity. She looks good in a skirt.'

Kay rolled her eyes, and followed Barnes.

Thankfully, the first responders had had the sense to set the cordon well back from the main tent where the CSI team were working, and she made a note to thank them for their foresight.

No doubt Suzie would be joined by several other reporters once word got out.

'Hunter.'

Sharp peered out from the tent and beckoned them over.

'How did the reporter get here so quick?' said Kay.

Sharp jerked his chin to one of the patrol cars, in the back of which sat an elderly man chatting to a female officer.

'Chap by the name of Harry Bertram was walking past to get his paper from the newsagent. Saw Powers sat in one of the cars outside the garage, and didn't like the look of it, so he wandered over to take a look. Once he got the door opened, he realised Powers was dead, so he told the newsagent to call us. Seems the newsagent rang a few more people, too.'

'Damn,' said Barnes. 'Did they get anything on camera before the screens went up?'

'No – the first responders were excellent – found those tarpaulins in the garage and got those strung up before the news team turned up.'

'The garage was unlocked?'

'Something we'll be looking into as part of the investigation, so add it to your list,' said Sharp.

'Okay, what happened to Powers?'

Sharp held the tent flap open.

Rather than enter the secure area, Kay and Barnes stood on the threshold.

There was no point in them all clamouring to see – they'd seen enough dead bodies in the past, and two more people traipsing around the crime scene wouldn't have been appreciated.

As it was, the stench of urine and shit mixed with

the trace of exhaust fumes, and Kay brought her sleeve to her nose to mask it.

'Asphyxiation,' said Sharp. 'Obviously, the post mortem will confirm it, but it's pretty obvious. An ambulance was sent out at the same time as the first responders, so they declared life extinct for us.'

Kay nodded. Having the ambulance crew confirm the death saved them dragging Lucas away from the mortuary and wasting time while they waited for him to arrive. At least Harriet and her team could work swiftly to preserve as much evidence as possible.

'Suicide?' said Barnes.

'I doubt it,' said Sharp. 'Not unless he pulled out his own fingernails before gassing himself.'

Barnes winced, and blew through his teeth.

'How'd his killer manage to asphyxiate him anyway?' said Kay. 'I thought that was difficult with modern cars.'

'This vehicle's over twenty years old,' said Sharp.

'The passenger window's cracked,' said Barnes.

'I'm working on the theory he kicked it to try to break the glass,' said Harriet as she brushed past one of her colleagues and wandered over. 'He's shifted in his seat slightly with his hips turned to the left, as if he's tried to use the heel of his boot to break it, but I'll firm up that once we've finished here. The cracks were certainly made from the inside of the car, not the outside.'

'How come he didn't open the door, if he could reach the window with his feet?' said Kay.

'The locks had been glued,' said Harriet. 'Bertram told your colleagues he had to break the driver's door open with a crowbar he found in the garage.'

She pulled her mask back up over her mouth and moved back to where her team worked, and Sharp let the tent flap drop back into place, then gestured to Kay and Barnes to follow him into the building.

The double doors at the front had been propped open, and another of Harriet's teams were studiously moving through the gloomy space within.

Sharp turned to Kay and Barnes, and lowered his voice.

'This is a direct result of Harrison's insistence on a press conference too early on in the investigation,' he said, his eyes blazing. 'There's no telling the damage he's done. How many more people are going to die before we find Demiri?'

Kay turned to face the road beyond the forecourt.

Two more vehicles had joined Suzie and her cameraman; different new channels clamouring for space along the narrow pavement.

Her heart skipped a beat as she recognised Jonathan Aspley, and she averted her gaze as he began to walk towards the cordon.

'Inspector!'

Harriet's voice carried across to where they were standing, her head poking out from the tent.

'What is it?' said Sharp.

'You need to see this.'

They hurried back to the covered area, and joined Harriet at the entrance.

'Come in,' she said. 'I don't want the risk of one of those news teams seeing this.'

They pushed into the cramped space, and Kay noticed the CSI's eyes were shining with excitement.

'What've you got?' said Barnes.

She beckoned them round to the driver's seat and crouched down. 'We noticed he had a piece of paper in his hand; we prised it open, and it looks like he used his own blood to leave a message.'

Kay felt a shiver crawl across her neck as Harriet handed the paper to Sharp.

As he took the corner between gloved fingers, his brow knitted together before he turned it to face them.

'A place and time,' he said. 'Mean anything to you two?'

'It's got to be Demiri's next shipment,' said Kay, her heart pounding. 'It's when he's bringing over the next lot of girls.'

# CHAPTER FORTY-SEVEN

'There's no time to plan this properly,' said Sharp through gritted teeth. 'It'll be a disaster.'

'No, it won't,' said Harrison. 'We'll have support from Border Agency and my SOCU team, plus uniformed officers.'

'With all due respect, guv, we've only got the name of a place. Not an exact location. He could be planning to land the boat anywhere along that stretch of coastline,' said Kay, and waved her hand at the document Sharp was reading. 'And, according to that email from the Border Agency, they want to base the majority of their team at Dymchurch because that's where previous smugglers have made landfall. We'll only have a handful of their officers available to support us.'

Harrison paced the room, his frustration palpable.

'Look,' he said eventually. 'There's enough of us to have four teams of four spread out at three-quarter-mile intervals. We maintain radio contact at all times. The weather forecast is showing rain, so we're not going to have as much visibility as I'd like, but we'll still be able to see a boat coming in; as it is, we'll be able to hear the engine before they cut it and drift to shore.'

'You think?' Sharp ran a hand over his jaw, and scratched at the stubble forming. 'I don't like it. It's too risky.'

'We don't have a choice, Sharp,' said Harrison. 'If we miss this boat, those girls are going to end up exactly like the ones we'd found dead. Do you want that on your conscience?'

Kay watched as her senior officer slumped in his seat, his eyes troubled.

'I thought not,' said Harrison. He picked up his jacket from the back of the visitor chair, and swung it over his shoulders. 'I'll go and brief headquarters and make the necessary phone calls to Colin Fox and his team at the Border Agency. We'll have a joint agency briefing here in the morning at eight o'clock, Sharp. Make sure your team is ready.'

He swept from the room, his hurried footsteps carrying through the incident room before Kay heard the door slam shut in his wake.

She pushed herself out of her chair and wandered over to the window, her arms folded over her chest.

Below, the DCI was walking towards his car, his phone to his ear.

'Start making phone calls to the rest of the team,' said Sharp. 'As well as yourself and Barnes, I want

Miles and Piper on that beach tomorrow night, and I don't want any issues so get them in early tomorrow – at least half an hour before the briefing's due to start, so we can make sure they understand the dangers involved.'

'Will do, guv.'

She turned at a knock on the open door.

'Lucas just emailed through the post mortem report on the three victims found at the property in Thurnham,' said Barnes. 'I printed out a copy for each of you.'

Sharp gestured to the seat vacated by Harrison moments earlier, and Barnes handed the paperwork over.

Kay flipped through the pages, her eyes taking in the detail of the torture the women had endured prior to being killed. The broken bones she and Sharp had noticed at the crime scene were horrific enough, but as she read the report, the extent of their internal injuries left a sickness in her stomach.

Barnes cleared his throat. 'As you'll see from Lucas's conclusions, he ascertains that all three victims' injuries were caused prior to their death.'

Kay exhaled and placed her copy on Sharp's desk.

Suddenly, any risks associated with the next night's operation paled in comparison to what would happen if Demiri wasn't apprehended and the illegal entrants rescued from the clutches of him and his men.

Kay paused at the door, and glanced over her shoulder.

'Given your military background and experience, I

have to say I'd be happier taking orders from you for this operation, guv.'

He shrugged, a weariness crossing his features that she hadn't seen before.

'It is what it is, Hunter. Go home and rest. It's going to be a long day tomorrow.'

# CHAPTER FORTY-EIGHT

Kay padded downstairs in her socks, her hair freshly washed. She wore her favourite pair of jeans and a baggy sweater, perfect for relaxing in front of the television with a glass of wine.

She reached out and flipped the thermostat up a notch, ensuring the central heating would counteract the cold wind that rattled the double glazed windows, and then made her way through to the kitchen.

Her two furry charges looked up at her from their hutch, hopeful expressions on their faces.

'I know, I know. Food time,' she said. She was surprised how quickly she had grown used to their presence in the house, and was secretly glad that the garden shed had proven to be too cluttered for their hutch.

She couldn't bear the thought of them having to brave the elements on the back patio, either.

She hummed to herself as she changed the soiled

newspapers, swapping them for clean ones and putting the rubbish outside before grabbing one of the bags of ready-chopped vegetables from the refrigerator.

Bonnie chattered to herself as Kay lifted Clyde from the hutch and gently applied ointment to his skin while he munched on a carrot top.

She turned him in her hands until the furry creature was facing her, and then held him up so they were eye to eye.

'You know what, Clyde? You two have a spoilt life. You don't have to worry about evil people. All you have to do is sit there and eat your carrots.'

Clyde wriggled his nose.

Kay smiled, lowered him back into the cage and secured the latch, and then washed her hands before helping herself to a large glass of wine while she prepared her own dinner.

As she worked, she gave a running commentary to the guinea pigs, then stopped abruptly.

'I'm losing the plot.'

She frowned, recognising her actions for what they were – a way of pushing the thought of tomorrow's operation to one side.

A sense of unease washed over her, and she shook her head as she served up the pasta onto a plate and pulled out a stool at the end of the worktop.

It would do no good to worry. DCI Harrison and his SOCU team were well versed in such matters, and they had support from the Border Agency and some of their own uniformed officers.

Still, a frisson of nerves and excitement sent a shiver down her spine.

Would Demiri be there?

Would she finally get the chance to arrest him?

She pushed her plate away, unable to stomach the food, realising she wouldn't be able to relax tonight, despite Sharp's advice.

She wandered over to the refrigerator and topped up her glass, then nearly dropped it when her mobile phone began to ring.

'Get a grip,' she muttered, and hurried back to the worktop. She smiled when she saw the caller's name.

'Hey, you.'

'Hello,' said Adam. 'Bad news, I'm afraid. The weather forecast isn't improving and they've cancelled my flight. It doesn't look like I'll be leaving here until tomorrow night now.'

'That's a pain. Have you managed to get in touch with the clinic?'

As Adam spoke about the various calls he'd made to his colleagues and the arrangements he'd made for his extended absence, Kay wondered if she should tell him about the planned operation for the following night.

After all, if Adam was home right now, she'd tell him.

Yet, he was over four hundred miles away, stranded with no way to get home, and it seemed unfair to give him any cause for concern.

She knew him too well – he would only worry – or do something drastic, like hire a car and drive home.

She bit her lip.

'So, what's happening there?' he said.

'All good. The investigation has been going well, and we're hoping to have a result soon.'

'You're staying away from trouble?'

She closed her eyes, thankful he hadn't said Demiri's name, and grateful she wouldn't have to lie.

'Yes.'

'Well, keep out of trouble for another twenty-four hours,' he said, and sighed. 'I can't believe I'm stuck up here tonight instead of being with you.'

'Don't worry,' said Kay. 'I'll be fine.'

## CHAPTER FORTY-NINE

Kay shoved her hands into her pockets and burrowed her face into the thick scarf she'd wrapped around her neck before leaving the station to drive to the coast.

She squinted in the fading moonlight as it scuttled behind clouds that obscured their view of the thrashing water of the English Channel pummelling the beach below.

Boots on sand sounded next to her, and Gavin appeared at her shoulder.

'Do you think he'll be here?'

She lifted her head and gasped at the cold wind that whipped at her face. She turned her back to the beach for a brief respite from the elements, and peered into the scrubby undergrowth that bordered the coast road.

'He'll be here. Somewhere. I can't imagine he'll want to lose his investment.'

Gavin grunted in response and glanced up at the sky.

'It's clouding over. Looks like we're going to get some more rain.'

Kay turned her attention back to the sea. 'It'll help him. We won't be able to spot the boat until it's almost here.'

'If we have the right place.'

'Where's Harrison?'

'About half a mile up that way.' Gavin pointed to their left. 'He's got teams spread out along the beach here, and into the next cove, just in case.'

'Carys and Barnes?'

'Beyond Harrison's position, by the next lot of groyne posts in the distance.'

Kay narrowed her eyes against the wind, catching a dark shadow at the end of the furthest post away from the water's edge. She glanced over her shoulder to the tumbledown cottage set back from the beach, its walls covered in ivy and its interior in darkness.

'No sign of the owner?'

'No. There's one of the free papers sticking out of the letterbox. Must be away. Barnes tried to rouse someone half an hour ago, but there's no response.'

'Shame. I'm surprised the DCI doesn't know the owner though. Thought he was keeping an eye on this part of the coastline.'

'Reckon it's one of Harrison's informants?'

Kay shivered. 'Rather his than Demiri's.'

They fell silent and turned back to the water.

Kay had wanted to question Harrison's orders that

the team split up along the length of the beach, but a sense of respect for Sharp made her hold her tongue.

She couldn't help feeling that she and Gavin were exposed so far from the rest of the team, but Harrison had been insistent and, in the end, she'd bit back her questions and resigned herself to a support role for the operation.

Her thoughts were interrupted by a tap on her arm from Gavin.

'Look.'

He pointed out to the darkened waters, and she followed his line of sight.

'I can't see anything.'

'I thought I saw something. Guess not.'

'This'd be so much easier if Fox's Border Agency lot were here.'

'Well, you heard him talking to Sharp and Harrison before we left the station. He was adamant he'd position his team further along the coast near Dymchurch, because that's where they've caught people before.'

'Yes – and it was all over the news when that happened, so I'm sure it's a "no-go" zone for people smugglers now.'

'I guess we have to try to cover as much as we can, Sarge.'

'I know. You're right. Be sod's law they *do* turn up along there, and—'

Kay heard Gavin's sharp intake of breath at the same time he held up his hand to silence her.

A low-slung vessel clung to the waves, approaching

the beach to the left of their position. The soft sound of its engine reached her, and her heartbeat ratcheted up a notch.

'It's them,' said Gavin.

Kay took the binoculars he handed to her.

In the weakened moonlight caused by the cloud cover, Kay could make out eight figures clinging to the sides, hunkered down against the elements.

In the middle of the small but powerful vessel, she could make out two thicker-set figures who had crouched next to the central steering column, trying to disguise their presence.

The dinghy crested a large wave, its stern lifting into the air before crashing over the next.

A cry could be heard over the noise of the sea, and Kay's heart went out to the young women, likely still in their teens and hundreds of miles from their homes and families, who had made the terrifying journey across one of the busiest shipping lanes in the world.

The engine revved once more, and then cut out as the dinghy was thrust towards the beach, the end of its voyage in sight.

'Sarge?' Gavin hissed.

Reluctantly, Kay handed back the binoculars, and bit her lip.

Harrison would have to time the apprehension of the vessel carefully.

Too soon, and the men piloting the craft would simply restart the engine and power away from the beach.

Worse, if they lost control or the engine died while the dinghy was mid-turn, it could mean disaster for everyone on board if one of the large waves struck at the same time, capsizing the boat.

Kay held her breath.

She had been reassured when Harrison's team had set up their vehicles towards the far end of the beach and pulled out thermal blankets and first aid kits. It was evident they were taking no chances, but if the occupants of the boat couldn't swim to safety in the perilous freezing water—

'There they go,' said Gavin.

Kay strained her eyes in the darkness, focusing in time to see the stern of the dinghy make landfall.

Seconds later, a dozen armed tactical response officers rose from their positions along the sand and raced towards it, yelling at the occupants to raise their hands in the air.

She edged forward, keen to be involved, then stopped as the radio clipped to her stab vest crackled to life.

Harrison's voice broke through the vicious static. 'All personnel not directly involved with the apprehension of the vessel, hold your positions.'

She heard Gavin emit a loud sigh.

'Always the bridesmaid, never the bride,' he grumbled.

# CHAPTER FIFTY

Kay squinted in the poor light.

Three of the Division's four-wheel-drive vehicles bounced over the scrubby plants that bordered the rough track before driving across the sand, heading towards the crowd gathering around the beached dinghy.

High-powered lights fixed to the roof of each vehicle flared to life illuminating the scene, and Kay swore profusely as she was temporarily blinded, despite being nearly a mile away.

'I can't hear a sodding thing through this,' Gavin muttered, and slapped the palm of his hand against the back of his radio. 'So much for being organised.'

Kay glanced across at him as the radio hissed in protest, then unhitched her own from her stab vest. 'Here.'

He took it from her, tucking his own down his vest, and tweaked the volume so they could listen to the reports from the other end of the beach.

Kay rocked forward on her toes, eager to be a more active part of the arrests.

'All other officers are to maintain position,' Harrison's voice cut through the static. 'We have Oliver Tavender in custody, but there's no sign of Demiri.'

'Dammit, he got away,' said Gavin.

'Shh. I'm trying to listen.'

She gestured to him to turn up the volume, but when he did so, it did little to improve the sound quality.

Frustrated, she scuffed her boots at the sand, obliterating their footprints.

She'd always preferred rocky beaches – places to scramble and climb over; fossils to discover; sea anemones that would cling to an outstretched finger if provoked.

Here, the landscape seemed more exposed and unforgiving – with nowhere to hide.

'So, where are you, Jozef?' she muttered.

'Sarge?'

'Nothing.'

She kicked at the sand a final time, then wandered over to where Gavin paced near the water's edge.

She blinked to try to stop her eyes watering from the wind and tugged her cap harder onto her head, before she became aware of footsteps in the soft sand behind her.

She spun around, her hands held up in a defensive position.

'Detective Hunter?'

'Mr Webster?'

She checked over her shoulder to see Gavin fiddling with the radio, a loud curse emanating from the young detective before he held the radio aloft and shrugged.

'This one's dead, too.'

She turned back to Webster.

The elderly man wore a weather-beaten anorak over jeans, his feet encased in a pair of old work boots and a woolly hat pulled low over his ears.

'Mr Webster, you need to return to your house for your own safety.'

He ignored her, and instead peered around her shoulder, his eyes flickering over Gavin before drifting to the scene beyond, then back to her.

'I think there's another boat,' he said, his eyes troubled. He reached out for her arm, and led her a few paces away before pointing to the darkened beach beyond.

'Over there. I left the house to see what all the commotion was, but as I was walking along the lane, I heard a voice call out, quietly.'

Kay's heart rate increased, and she moved closer to the old man to try to see what he was pointing at.

'Where?'

'See that groyne post, about quarter of a mile long? Behind there.'

'Gav?'

'Sarge?'

'Any luck with that radio?'

'No.' He spat out the word.

Kay pulled out her mobile phone, and bit her lip.

Harrison's instructions had been clear – no mobile phones, for fear of the light from the screen or an errant ring tone alerting anyone to their presence.

She stared at the darkened screen a moment longer, then shoved it back into her vest.

'Dammit.'

It would go against all her training, but she couldn't let Demiri get away. She ran through the risks in her head, discarding them one by one.

'Gav? We're going to need backup, so get yourself over to Sharp and bring back a team to help us.'

'What are you going to do?'

'I'm going to get a bit closer, and get Mr Webster to show me where this dinghy is.'

'Sarge, with all due respect, it'd be better to wait. You can't go on your own.'

She lowered her voice. 'I'm not letting him get away. I'll keep my distance. Go – you'll be less than ten minutes, right?'

He nodded, his face miserable. 'I still don't like it, Sarge.'

'We're wasting time talking about it. Go!'

She watched as Gavin turned and began to jog away, his gait awkward on the sand, and then turned to Webster.

'Show me.'

'It's over here,' said Webster. 'This way.'

For an older man, Webster set a steady pace across

the beach away from the lights of the border agency vehicle and into the gloom beyond.

'Slow down,' Kay hissed.

'Sorry,' said Webster. 'I guess I'm used to walking along here. I forget you're not local.'

Kay gestured to him to continue, the roar of the surf obliterating any other noise around her.

As the row of groyne posts came into view, she reached out and placed her hand on Webster's shoulder.

'Wait.'

To her right, she could make out the outline of Webster's cottage across the track from the beach. No lights shone in the windows, and she wondered how often the man found that sleep eluded him and chose to walk the beach at night instead.

'I can't see a dinghy.'

He put a finger to his lips. 'It's just the other side of the groyne posts,' he said. 'And, keep your voice down. Sound travels better near water.'

Kay frowned, unable to believe that anything could be heard over the noise of the wind and surf that was currently battling her ears.

She felt the weight of her mobile phone, safe in its pocket in her stab vest, and wondered whether it was worth the risk to switch it on and send Sharp a text message to let him know that she was within striking distance of the boat that Webster said he had seen. She discarded the thought almost immediately, knowing that if Demiri escaped because he'd seen the light from her mobile phone, she'd never hear the end of it from either Harrison or his superiors.

Gavin was nowhere to be seen.

She felt Webster slip from her grasp.

'Come on,' he said. 'I'll show you where it is.'

She stumbled after Webster, spray from the surf blinding her temporarily as the wind tugged at her hair.

Webster dropped into a crouch as they drew closer to the groyne posts and beckoned to her.

Silently, she followed him, wondering where Gavin was, but determined that Demiri wouldn't get away.

She checked over her shoulder again, but still no-one followed in her wake. Turning back, she emitted a surprised cry.

Webster was nowhere in sight.

'Mr Webster?'

She pushed her hair out of her eyes, then slipped an elastic band off her wrist and tied it back. The old man was nowhere to be seen in the darkness, and her heart skipped a beat.

She edged around the groyne posts, fully expecting to see another dinghy laden with women who had risked everything to cross the English Channel.

Her breath caught in her throat, confusion seizing her.

The beach was empty. She straightened, her thoughts tumbling over one another as she tried to comprehend what was going on. She sensed movement behind her, and spun on her heel a moment before a fist slammed into her face.

As she lay gasping on the soft sand, she raised a shaking hand to her bleeding lip, before a shadow stood over her.

'Hello, Detective Hunter,' said Jozef Demiri. 'I've been waiting for you.'

# CHAPTER FIFTY-ONE

Gavin's boots pummelled the sand, his breath fogging in front of his face as he ran towards the floodlit scene at the far end of the beach.

Already, he regretted leaving Kay behind, but she was his senior officer and her tone had suggested she wasn't in the mood to debate with him.

He paused, his chest heaving, and glanced over his shoulder.

Kay and Webster were nowhere to be seen, their figures lost to the darkness.

He swore, then took off again, cursing the loose surface under his feet. Although at home by the sea and an avid surfer at any opportunity, he was used to running across it in bare feet, not regulatory lace up boots. The leather uppers and sturdy rubber soles weighed him down, making his footsteps sluggish.

As he drew closer, his eyes scanned the crowd for one of his colleagues.

Two uniformed officers were helping the bedraggled women from the dinghy.

The women were no older than early twenties, their bodies emaciated, the terrified expressions belying their confusion at being arrested instead of escaping to the better life Demiri and his men had no doubt promised.

'Out of the way.'

An older uniformed officer brushed past him, his hand on a woman's elbow as he guided her towards one of the waiting vehicles now parked on the track above the beach. As they pushed past, the woman threw a pleading look at Gavin, but he shook his head.

He had to find Sharp, or one of the others, and fast.

He craned his neck over the crowd surrounding the tiny vessel, and finally caught sight of Carys talking to Barnes and their DI as she helped one of the other women out of the boat, keeping hold of her hand while she stumbled onto the sand.

Gavin elbowed his way through the crowd, earning several dirty looks and exclamations of annoyance.

He didn't care.

'Sharp! Sir!' he called as he drew closer.

His voice carried away by the wind and chatter around him, he reached the stern of the dinghy and realised he couldn't get any closer.

The crowd was too big.

He stuck his forefinger and thumb into his mouth and blew a whistle so loud, the man next to him visibly jumped.

Ignoring his glare, Gavin took advantage of the brief, shocked silence.

'Sharp, sir! It's Hunter!'

His senior officer didn't hesitate. He slapped Barnes on the shoulder, pushed Carys ahead of him, and shoved his way through the other officers until he reached Gavin.

'What's wrong?'

'Adrian Webster appeared at our position further along the beach. Says he thinks he saw another dinghy. We couldn't raise anyone on our radios, and Hunter didn't want to phone you because of our operational orders.'

Sharp flapped his hand impatiently. 'Where's Hunter now?'

'She ordered me to come and get you and a few others. She's gone with Webster to find the other dinghy.'

'She did what?'

Sharp turned and waved over the crowd to where Harrison stood talking to one of his SOCU colleagues.

The DCI's head jerked up, and he hurried over, O'Reilly at his heels.

'Good work everyone. Time for congratulating yourselves later, though—'

'Hunter's gone in search of another suspected dinghy,' said Sharp, already edging away. He turned his attention to Gavin, Barnes and Carys. 'All of you – with me, now.'

Harrison frowned. 'What's the rush?'

'Had you heard of Adrian Webster before he had phoned the hotline following the press conference?'

'No, I—'

'Then, he's not one of your informants?'

'No. Is that a problem?'

'It means he's one of Demiri's. Kay's been set up.'

Harrison's eyes widened. 'Demiri's here?'

O'Reilly placed a hand on Harrison's sleeve. 'Let's get him.'

Gavin's heart missed a beat, his attention snapping to the DS. 'What did you say?'

O'Reilly took a step back, a look of fear crossing his face for a moment before he recovered. 'What do you mean?'

'It was *you*,' Gavin snarled, and launched himself at the other detective.

O'Reilly stumbled backwards, his hands raising in a defensive position, but it did him no good.

Gavin's fist found the man's face with a satisfying crunch, seconds before O'Reilly howled in pain.

'Piper!'

Gavin became aware of Sharp's voice through the sound of blood rushing in his ears, and reined back his next strike, panting.

A hand on his shoulder spun him round, and Sharp's grey eyes bore into him.

'You've got thirty seconds to explain yourself, Piper.'

Gavin swallowed, Sharp's tone reminding him that the DI had spent his pre-police years on a military parade ground, barking orders. He glanced over his shoulder, to see O'Reilly staggering to his feet, aided by Harrison.

The DS wore a hunted expression, and Gavin sneered at him before turning back to Sharp.

'O'Reilly was one of the men who beat me up earlier this year,' he said. 'I recognise his voice now.'

Sharp took a step back. 'Twenty seconds left.'

'When they pounced on me in the car park that night, just before they laid into me, I heard one of them say to the other "let's get him". Exactly how O'Reilly said it just now. It's why when Kay asked to see the CCTV footage of the attack, O'Reilly told her there wasn't much to see – he'd obviously got hold of the recording and edited it before showing it to anyone. Only two men could be seen in the video, but there were three men there. O'Reilly stayed in the shadows, but I know it was him.'

Sharp peered around Gavin's shoulder. 'Is this true, O'Reilly?'

Dead silence met his words, and Gavin clenched his fists at the realisation that one of their own had ensured he'd been made to suffer.

But why?

He caught the stricken expression that crossed Carys's face as she grasped what she was hearing, and that the detective sergeant she'd placed on a pedestal was responsible for the attack on her colleague.

'O'Reilly, get yourself over to the ambulance and

sort that nose out. Harrison – we'll deal with this later,' said Sharp. 'Right now, one of my officers is in danger.'

He turned and took off at a sprint, the rest of the team at his heels.

'Where did she go, Piper?'

'There's a row of groyne posts about quarter of a mile from our original position. Webster told us he'd seen a dinghy there.'

Carys drew level with them, the sound of Barnes's heavy breathing several paces behind.

'Guv? Kay isn't a strong swimmer. We did our refresher training together. She can't hold her breath underwater for long.'

Sharp said nothing, and they began to run faster.

# CHAPTER FIFTY-TWO

Kay's throat constricted.

Jozef Demiri towered over her, his white hair hidden under a dark woollen hat, a thick coat covering his shoulders protecting him from the elements.

He took a step back, and Kay began to struggle upright.

His boot connected with her knee before she could react.

Pain scorched through the joint, and Kay screamed, collapsing onto the sand as tears pricked her eyelids.

She hugged her hands around her knee and tried to think how long Gavin had been gone, and how long it might be until he returned with Sharp.

She gulped back a sob as she realised he might not find her.

They'd only had Webster's vague description of where the supposed dinghy was, and she'd sent Gavin for reinforcements before Webster had provided more detail.

And all the while he'd been leading her into danger.

Demiri moved close, his heavy breathing reaching her ears over the noise of the surf.

At first, she thought he was out of breath, hobbled by age and the effort to move on the sand.

Then the realisation hit her with a fresh wave of sickness.

He was enjoying her torment.

'Why now, Demiri?' she spat. 'We'd lost you. Why run and hide, only to show yourself now?'

He crouched next to her, the soft denim of his jeans brushing against her cheek, and she flinched before cursing her reaction.

'I didn't run and hide, bitch,' he said. 'I waited. For you. Your persistence will destroy you, Detective Hunter. You destroyed my business. I will destroy your life. Piece by piece.'

He straightened, his eyes never leaving hers.

'I knew all I'd have to do was wait. Leave you a trail of breadcrumbs you wouldn't be able to resist.'

'Why Webster?'

'Why not? The man was paid well. He provided me with somewhere to stay. I must say, detective, it excited me when you were sent to meet him after our phone call to your so-called hotline. I could hear your voice, and wondered what you would do if you knew I was there, listening to you, so close to where you sat in his living room, listening to his lies. He did well to lay the trap for you, and you fell for it like a fool.'

Kay groaned.

He was right, of course. Because Webster had been the one so eager to help the police and report suspicious activities on the beach, she'd trusted him.

Trusted him enough to follow him blindly into Demiri's trap.

'You'll never get away with it.'

The shock at hearing the fear in her own voice turned to anger as she saw the effect it had on him.

He bared his teeth.

Kay clawed at Demiri's hands as he reached down and grabbed the front of her stab vest and began to drag her towards the churning surf.

Despite his age, the man possessed an enormous strength, and lifted her with ease.

Her thoughts returned to the evidence he and his men had left behind in the nightclub cellar, and she fought down the urge to be sick.

She had to slow him down. She had to hope Gavin and the rest of the team were close by.

She opened her mouth to yell, to call out, to let them know where she was, but before she could, Demiri paused in his tracks and slapped her across the face.

She gasped with the shock of the impact, and then he was dragging her once more.

She dug her heels into the wet sand, desperately trying to slow him down, to delay what she knew was going to happen.

Her thoughts turned to her compulsory training, the extra swimming lessons that gained her a pass but did nothing to quell her fear of water.

Demiri's fetid breath swept over her face as he worked, and then suddenly she was falling. She screamed as her arm twisted at an impossible angle with the force of the impact, and then seawater filled her mouth and nostrils.

A weight landed on her legs, and a hand gripped her stab vest as once more she was hauled from the surf coughing and spluttering.

Eyes stinging, her left arm useless at her side, she turned her head and vomited from her sitting position.

A large wave smacked against her spine, fanning out across her shoulders and splashing Demiri's face.

She was shivering uncontrollably now, and struggled to focus on the large hands that held her.

Her head dropped forward, her chin resting on his knuckles as she tried to gulp in precious air.

'Look at me!'

Demiri shook her until she turned her eyes to him.

Every time she'd imagined arresting the organised crime boss, she'd imagined feeling victorious, casting a blow to the crime community, and being hailed a heroine by the same people who had tried to destroy her career.

Now, she realised she'd underestimated him badly, and she was absolutely terrified.

Demiri raised her up by the stab vest until their faces were almost touching.

She could feel the hatred emanating from him, a pure evil that crawled over her shoulders and loosened her bowels.

At that moment, she knew she was going to die.

# CHAPTER FIFTY-THREE

Gavin glanced to his left as Sharp slowed, then realised the DI was reaching into his utility belt for his torch, and followed suit.

Kay's safety was more important than Harrison's operational requirements.

Carys and Barnes caught up with them, and Sharp held up his hand to stop them forging ahead.

'We walk the rest of the way. We don't know Demiri is there for sure, and we only have Webster's word that there's a second dinghy.'

'She's in trouble, guv,' said Barnes. 'I can feel it.'

'All the more reason that we don't go rushing in there like fools. It could be a trap.'

'What's the plan?' said Carys.

'We fan out,' said Sharp. 'I want you evenly spaced between the shoreline and the road. That leaves about twelve foot between us, so we know no-one can try to leave the beach without us seeing them. Keep your torch beams on the sand in front of you, sweeping from left to right. We know our target is the groyne posts over there, so keep going. If I say stop, you stop. This is no time for heroics.'

They jogged into position and kept moving forward, and Gavin found himself with Sharp to his left and Carys closest to the unpaved road that ran the length of the beach. He could just make out Barnes, closer to the surf.

A sickness engulfed him, and he wished he'd insisted on staying with Kay. He knew he'd done the right thing by following orders and that she'd have gone anyway, but the sense of dread had been growing since he first told Sharp what had happened.

His thoughts returned to Carys's comment that Kay wasn't a strong swimmer. He knew the churning waters would make swimming dangerous, not only because of the cold but also the risk of being carried away by a rip current.

And if she couldn't hold her breath for long—

The wind tugged at his cap, and then the roar of an engine reached his ears. Without slowing down, he glanced over his shoulder and saw two uniformed vehicles speeding along the road to catch up with them, lights blazing.

A figure stumbled towards them, silhouetted against the vehicles' headlights, and he recognised the gangly figure of the DCI.

Evidently, Harrison was more alarmed at his news than he first thought, and he picked up his pace.

'Easy, Piper,' said Sharp. 'We'll find her.'

'That's a tactical response vehicle,' said Gavin.

'I know. That's good. It means they're taking your message seriously. And all the more reason not to go running across there. Demiri could have a gun.'

Gavin swallowed.

The thought that Demiri might have a weapon hadn't even crossed his mind, and he cursed himself for doubting Sharp. He turned his attention to the cottage set back from the beach.

Adrian Webster had played them all.

Gavin was in no doubt that the man was an informant of Demiri's, as Sharp had suggested.

'This is where I left her with Webster,' he said to Sharp. He pointed out the groyne posts, still quarter of a mile away.

'Try her on the radio,' said Sharp.

'I can't.'

'What? Why not?'

'My radio wasn't working when we tried to call you for back up, so Hunter gave me hers.'

Sharp stopped dead in his tracks. 'She did what?'

'The radios are useless, guv. Hers didn't work either, and like I said – she didn't want to switch on her mobile phone because of Harrison's orders. She didn't want to alert Demiri or anyone else to us being here.'

Sharp peered along the road to where the vehicles were powering towards them.

'They're not going to get here in time.'

He began to run towards the groyne posts, the rest of them ignoring his orders to fan out and instead following in his wake.

As he ran, Gavin knew he'd never forgive himself for leaving Kay behind.

He should have stayed.

He should have insisted on accompanying Webster instead, while Kay sought help.

He should have—

'Stop it, Piper.'

Sharp's words cut through his thoughts.

'Guv?'

'Stop blaming yourself. You were given a direct order by a superior officer. You acted on it.'

'I was wrong.'

'No, you weren't.'

'Sharp!'

Gavin slowed to a walk as Harrison staggered towards them, breathing heavily.

The DCI held up a hand to shield his eyes from their torch beams. 'Any sign of Hunter?'

'Nothing. Why didn't your comms team check the radios were working properly?'

Harrison frowned. 'There's nothing wrong with the radios.'

Sharp narrowed his eyes, but jerked his thumb over his shoulder. 'Hunter was meant to be heading that way.'

'What about Demiri?'

'Haven't seen him yet, either.'

'Who the hell is that?'

Gavin spun round at Cary's voice, in time to see a shadowy figure lurching across the sand, away from the direction of the groyne posts.

'Webster,' he growled.

Movement to his left caught him off guard, and then Barnes was sprinting up the beach towards Webster, clearing the space between them with surprising speed for a man of his size.

They all followed, Gavin leading the way, but he didn't make it in time.

Barnes launched himself at the man, sending the two of them tumbling to the sand.

Webster cried out, then wiggled out from under Barnes and began to crawl away.

Barnes reached out and grabbed hold of the man's ankle, using his weight to pin Webster down while he scrambled to stop him escaping.

'Barnes, no!'

Barnes ignored the shout from Sharp. He wrapped his fingers around the man's coat and shook him.

'Where is she? Where's Hunter?'

A hand grabbed his shoulder and hauled him off Webster, a low voice in his ear.

'Hey,' said Gavin.

Barnes shrugged his shoulder to loosen the younger detective's grip, and glared at Webster, who was still lying on the sand, his eyes gleaming in the light from their torches.

Suddenly, a piercing scream cut through the darkness.

Carys whimpered at Sharp's side.

'What have you done with Kay?' said Gavin.

The old man cackled.

'You're too late. Demiri has her.'

# CHAPTER FIFTY-FOUR

Demiri's white hair blew wildly around his weathered features, his black eyes blazing a second before he spat in Kay's face.

'You think you are better than me, don't you Detective Hunter?'

He shifted position, his legs straddling hers as he ran his eyes over her body. 'You insult me. You underestimated me. You're too stupid to ever comprehend the power I command. The people who answer to me.'

Kay took a deep breath and closed her eyes a moment before he thrust her under the waves once more.

The back of her head hit the closely packed sand, knocking the breath she'd been so desperate to hold out of her.

Tears pricked her eyes as she raised her right hand and reached out blindly. She scratched Demiri's face, trying to work out where the man's eyes and nose were – soft, easy targets in a normal defensive situation, but impossible while fighting underwater.

A tightness in her chest began to grip her – a sudden urge to open her mouth and seek out oxygen, but her instincts were screaming at her that to do so would mean certain death.

Suddenly, she was hauled upwards once more, and the cold fresh wind slapped her face a split second before Demiri's fist punched her in the stomach.

He let go of his grip on her stab vest, and she tumbled onto the wet sand, gasping, her belly on fire.

Her vision began to weaken, black spots appearing at the edges of her line of sight.

'I think that's enough fun for one day.'

Demiri's voice sounded close by, and Kay rolled over onto her stomach and tried to raise herself on shaking legs.

She collapsed, breaking her fall with her good arm, and began to crawl away, shocked by the sound of her own sobs.

She didn't want to die.

Not now.

Not here.

Not like this.

Her arm was swept out from under her, a brutal kick that sent her sprawling onto the sand, and then he was dragging her towards the waves once more.

'No. Please.'

She dug her heels into the sand, trying to slow him, and slapped at the hands that held her vest.

She spat sand from her mouth, her breath escaping in wheezing, ragged gasps.

Her heart beat painfully and she stared in terror as the water drew nearer, unable to escape the clutches of the man who held her.

He stopped at the water's edge, and looked down at her, contempt filling his features.

'Time to die, Detective Hunter.'

'No – wait!'

Pain shot through her body as Demiri's weight landed on her, his hands moving from her vest to her throat as the water covered her face.

A roaring filled her ears, and an ache filled her heart as she wondered fleetingly which of her colleagues would have to inform Adam of her death at the hands of a man she had been hunting for nearly two years.

She could sense the exhaustion overwhelming her, a tiredness that was becoming too tempting to ignore.

Her lungs burned with the effort to hold her breath, her throat crushed within Demiri's grip.

A sound reached her ears – a muffled crack that pierced through her thoughts, and then the weight on her chest was gone, and she welcomed the darkness that engulfed her.

## CHAPTER FIFTY-FIVE

The fog cleared, and as her eyes focused, Kay noticed a familiar figure sitting in the chair next to her bed, his attention on a book in his lap.

'Guv?'

Sharp's head jerked up before his face softened, the skin around his eyes crinkling. He didn't look like he'd got any sleep for a while.

'Adam said you'd probably wake up the moment he went to get us some coffee.'

'Where am I?'

'Folkestone Hospital. Closest one we could get you to, in the circumstances.'

Bright sunlight shone through the slats of white window blinds and bathed the room in a soft hue.

Kay ran her tongue over her lips, the tip making contact with a scab on her top lip.

She frowned. 'What day is it?'

'Thursday. You've been out of it for a couple of days. Nothing serious. They kept you sedated as a precaution. You've got a nasty bump on your head, and there was concern you might have been suffering from hypothermia.'

Kay raised her left hand to feel the back of her skull, confusion sweeping over her at the weight of her arm before she realised it was covered in plaster.

She shivered as a memory resurfaced.

'Your doctor says it's a clean break. No metalwork involved,' said Sharp. 'A bit of physiotherapy once that's off, and you'll be on the mend.'

'Demiri?'

He cleared his throat. 'He won't be bothering you again. He's dead.'

'What happened?'

'Harrison shot him.'

Kay blinked. 'What?'

She clumsily tried to raise herself, until Sharp took pity on her, stood up and arranged the pillows behind her until she could sit comfortably.

Her brow remained creased as her mind tried to process his news.

'How—'

'He used Demiri's gun.'

'O'Reilly.' Kay spat out the word, and closed her eyes, the sound of footsteps reaching her ears.

'Not the response I was expecting.'

She opened her eyes and turned her attention to where Sharp stood, peering through the blinds.

He let the plastic slats snap back into place, then raised an eyebrow in her direction.

Kay lowered her gaze and dropped her hand to the blanket, then exhaled. She owed Sharp the truth, and nothing less.

'When I started my own investigation in the spring, before Gavin was attacked, I logged into the database. The entry for the gun that had been logged into evidence before being removed was missing. I managed to use my administration rights to find out who'd deleted it, and O'Reilly's name showed up. When I double-checked the system two days later to continue my investigation, that administration record had been deleted, too. It was like O'Reilly's name had never existed.'

Sharp shoved his hands into his pockets. 'And you didn't think to raise this with me at the time?'

'I had no proof!'

Kay swallowed, her throat still coarse from the salt water.

Sharp noticed her discomfort and filled a glass with water from a jug on the bedside table and handed it to her.

'Thanks,' she said, and drained the contents while Sharp lowered himself into the chair once more.

He took the glass from her then eased back into the seat and ran a hand over his face.

'O'Reilly was the one who organised the attack on Gavin to scare you off.'

'What? Wh—? Were he and Harrison working for Demiri?'

'No. Thank God. The fallout from this is going to be bad enough as it is.'

'Then, why?'

'Same as removing the gun from evidence and blaming it on you, I expect. Ambition,' said Sharp.

'So, O'Reilly removes the gun from evidence, Harrison then deletes the record of it ever existing, and O'Reilly arranges to beat up Gavin because I used his computer to find out about the gun,' she said, then frowned. 'What was in it for O'Reilly?'

Sharp had recovered, and rose from the chair, pacing the room as he spoke.

'Fast track promotion to DCI,' he said. 'Harrison decided he wanted Demiri for himself. He didn't want my team to be the one to charge Demiri. It would've ruined his plans to run a major undercover investigation and arrest Demiri for a massive drug operation. Harrison was more or less guaranteed a promotion to Detective Superintendent if he succeeded.'

Kay blinked, the room spinning, and slumped back against the pillows, her hand shaking.

'Are you okay?'

She shook her head, stunned. 'Not really. Run that by me again.'

'DCI Harrison states he was concerned that your investigation was about to expose Gareth Jenkins's position within Demiri's organisation, and in his own words "arranged to take drastic action" to protect Jenkins. Gareth's fingerprints were also on that weapon, and if you'd pursued your enquiries with the same diligence you'd demonstrated up to that point, you'd have blown apart a two-year undercover operation of his.'

Kay brought her hand to her mouth, bewildered. 'I lost my daughter.'

'I'm aware of that,' Sharp said quietly. 'I'm so sorry, Kay.'

'Not good enough,' Kay snapped, sitting upright. She glared at the DI. 'Do you have any idea the stress he put me through? Do you know what it's like to wake up in the middle of the night crying, because the tiny being you were carrying isn't kicking anymore? Do you know what it's like to have to pack away all the baby clothes and toys you'd bought because the doctors said there'd be no more children? And then, to have to return to work knowing none of your colleagues trust you anymore, even though you've been cleared of any wrongdoing?'

She reached across to a box of tissues on the bedside table next to her, swiped two and blew her nose with one before dabbing at her eyes with the other, then turned back to Sharp.

Her next words died on her tongue.

He appeared as distraught as she, his face white as he met her gaze.

'You really didn't know, did you?'

He shook his head.

'Those girls...' Kay cleared her throat. 'Didn't

Harrison care how many more died because of his actions?'

'Harrison maintains he didn't know about Demiri's sick killing club until Jenkins told us before he died.'

'Then why shoot Demiri? Why not arrest him?'

He shrugged. 'I guess we'll have to wait and see what Professional Standards find out. Maybe it frightened him, knowing that he was about to lose another officer on his watch.'

'Does Adam know about this?'

Sharp nodded. 'I arranged for a car to meet him at Heathrow the moment the ambulance was taking you to the hospital,' he explained. 'Carys told me you'd mentioned to her that his flight had been delayed, and I wanted to get him here as fast as I could. We thought we'd lost you, Kay.'

His voice broke.

Kay looked away, uncomfortable at his genuine concern.

'I don't understand why Demiri didn't simply escape the country,' she said eventually. 'We nearly lost him, guv. Why stay? Why wait to confront me?'

'We can only assume he became obsessed about you,' said Sharp. 'As you did with him, wanting to see him put away for what he'd done.'

'What about the cameras and listening devices in my house?'

'Definitely Demiri's work. Harrison states neither he nor O'Reilly had anything to do with those.'

'You believe them?'

'They looked absolutely petrified when it was put to them.'

Kay sighed and let her head rest back on the pillows once more. Her head ached, and not just from the bruising she'd sustained when Demiri had banged her skull against the hard, wet sand.

There was too much to comprehend.

Too much treachery.

'Hang on,' she said, jerking upright once more. 'Why you?'

Sharp stopped pacing. 'What?'

'Why has Harrison been targeting *your* team? What's his problem?'

He didn't answer, and Kay narrowed her eyes.

'Wha—'

Sharp held up his hand to silence her as the door to the room opened and Adam entered, his hands wrapped around two takeaway coffee cups.

He nearly dropped them in his haste to cross to the bed, and handed the drinks to Sharp before enveloping Kay in a hug.

She savoured his embrace, closing her eyes and pushing away the sudden flashback of her terror at being held underwater by Demiri, sure she was going to die.

Right here, right now, she was safe, and with the one person who mattered most in her life.

Adam broke off his hug as Sharp cleared his throat, and pulled across a second visitor chair to the side of the bed, wrapping his fingers around Kay's free hand.

'I wanted to wait until you were both here to do

this,' said Sharp. He reached into the inside of his jacket and extracted a white envelope before holding it out.

'Guv?'

'Take it.'

She reached out with a shaking hand, turning the envelope over. Her eyes met Adam's.

'Help me open it?'

He ran his thumb under the flap and eased out the folded page within until she could grasp it in her right hand.

She paused a moment, wondering if this was when her whole career came crashing down, a request for her resignation surely the only option open to her superiors after the events of two nights ago.

She sniffed, then unfolded the page and ran her eyes over the black text.

The words blurred, and she wiped at her eyes before she tried again, and then gasped.

*Your promotion to Detective Inspector has been recommended and approved.*

Her hand shook as she dropped the letter to her lap.

'I can't accept this, guv.'

She heard Adam's sudden intake of breath, but kept her eyes on Sharp.

'Can I ask why not?'

'It's become too political. All I wanted was to be a good detective. I saw what was going on between you and Harrison. The rivalry. With all due respect, guv, I don't want to be a part of that. I just want to get on with the job.'

'At least think about it,' he said, and then fell silent as the door to the private room opened once more.

Kay frowned; two uniformed officers entered the room, followed by DCI Angus Larch, his eyes blazing.

'I should have known I'd find you here, Sharp. Detective Sergeant Hunter, I'm sorry to intrude.' He didn't wait for her to respond. Instead, he turned his attention back to her senior officer. 'Detective Inspector Sharp, I'm here to relieve you of all duties pending a Professional Standards investigation into your conduct as a senior police officer.'

Adam's grip on her hand tightened before a sickness crawled into Kay's stomach, her heart racing as her eyes shifted from Larch to Sharp. 'What's going on, guv?'

Sharp's jaw worked, and he moved to where he'd placed his jacket on the other visitor chair. He shrugged it over his shoulders before lifting his gaze to meet hers. 'I'll explain when I can. But you're right. The rivalry and the politics don't make it an easy job.'

Larch watched as Sharp was led away by the two uniformed officers before turning back to Kay.

'You surpassed even your own stupidity this time,' he said. He held up a hand to stop her interrupting, and pointed at the page in her lap. 'And if you think you're going to take on that promotion, you can think again. Until I say so otherwise, you're *acting* Detective Inspector while this whole mess involving Sharp has been cleared up. One way or the other.'

'What will happen to him?'

Larch pursed his lips, then shrugged. 'I'm not sure.

Obviously, he has an exemplary record for successful investigations, and that will be taken into consideration.'

Adam collapsed into his chair, and ran his hand over his mouth. 'I can't believe it. I—'

Kay reached out until her hand found his.

'On the understanding this doesn't leave this room, Sharp was assisting Professional Standards with an investigation into Harrison's methods of running cases,' said Larch. He contemplated his fingernails. 'All I'm prepared to say is that it seems Harrison used some less than savoury methods to conclude his investigations. On the other hand, Harrison has made some serious accusations about Sharp, and those accusations have to be fully investigated.'

'God, what a mess,' said Adam.

Kay said nothing, but thought back to the meeting she'd had with Jonathan Aspley, and wondered if the journalist had anything to do with Larch's admission.

What had happened between Harrison and Sharp to cause such animosity?

Would Aspley ever tell her if he'd uncovered more about Harrison than he had previously told her?

Larch cleared his throat, interrupting her thoughts. 'Anyway, I'll let you two have some privacy.'

Kay waited until the door had closed behind him before she spoke.

'Sharp tell you about what O'Reilly and Harrison did?'

'Yeah. Honestly, Kay – I thought you were going to

find out Larch was responsible for all of it. He seemed the type.'

She shook her head, and managed a small smile. 'No. He's just one of life's career arseholes.'

Adam snorted.

'Listen, don't blame Sharp for any of this. It's my own fault. I was the one who kept pushing to go after Demiri. I was the one who wanted to be a part of the raid on the beach.'

'Don't make excuses for any of them, Kay. Don't.' Tears shone in his eyes, and he wiped at them with the sleeve of his shirt. 'After all we've been through since they blamed you for the missing evidence.'

'Sharp is innocent, Adam. Whatever's going on, he has to be innocent. He's always looked out for me before, whenever he can.'

He reached out for her once more, and shook his head, a sad smile on his face. 'You opened a can of worms this time, Hunter.'

She squeezed his hand, closed her eyes and sighed, exhausted.

'I *knew* there'd be hell to pay.'


<<<< THE END >>>>

# FROM THE AUTHOR

Dear Reader,

First of all, I wanted to say a huge thank you for choosing to read *Hell to Pay*. I hope you enjoyed the story.

If you did enjoy it, I'd be grateful if you could write a review. It doesn't have to be long, just a few words, but it is the best way for me to help new readers discover one of my books for the first time.

If you'd like to stay up to date with my new releases, as well as exclusive competitions and giveaways, you're welcome to join my Reader Group at my website, www.rachelamphlett.com. I will never share your email address, and you can unsubscribe at any time.

You can also contact me via Facebook, Twitter, or by email. I love hearing from readers – I read every message and will always reply.

Thanks again for your support.

Best wishes,

Rachel Amphlett

CPSIA information can be obtained
at www.ICGtesting.com
Printed in the USA
LVHW02s0511211217
560400LV00004B/1048/P

9 780994 547941